Katherine Saw Him Just as She Reached for the Champagne.

Her fingers closed around the cool crystal glass as she turned away. But even then, though she didn't allow herself to look his way, she felt the terrible force of Rashid Ben Hasir's stare and knew that he had moved toward her.

"It's been a long time," he said. "Six years?"

"Seven."

She had forgotten how tall he was, how dark his eyes were. His black hair had touches of silver now and so did the moustache that he had not had before.

"What are you doing in Rabat?" His words were more than just a question; they were a challenge.

Dear Reader:

There is an electricity between two people in love that makes everything they do magic, larger than life. This is what we bring you in SILHOUETTE INTIMATE MOMENTS.

SILHOUETTE INTIMATE MOMENTS are longer, more sensuous romance novels filled with adventure, suspense, glamor or melodrama. These books have an element no one else has tapped: excitement.

We are proud to present the very best romance has to offer from the very best romance writers. In the coming months look for some of your favorite authors such as Elizabeth Lowell, Nora Roberts, Erin St. Claire and Brooke Hastings.

SILHOUETTE INTIMATE MOMENTS are for the woman who wants more than she has ever had before. These books are for you.

Karen Solem
Editor-in-Chief
Silhouette Books

Bedouin Bride

Barbara Faith

Silhouette Intimate Moments

Published by Silhouette Books New York

America's Publisher of Contemporary Romance

Silhouette Books by Barbara Faith

The Promise of Summer (IM #16)
Wind Whispers (IM #47)
Bedouin Bride (IM #63)

SILHOUETTE BOOKS, a Division of Simon & Schuster, Inc.
1230 Avenue of the Americas, New York, N.Y. 10020

Distributed by Pocket Books

ISBN: 0-671-47125-2

First Silhouette Books printing August, 1984

10 9 8 7 6 5 4 3 2 1

America's Publisher of Contemporary Romance

Printed in the U.S.A.

For Chet Cunningham
and the San Diego nitpickers

Of the lands of North Africa the Arabs have a saying: "Algeria is a man, Tunisia a woman, Morocco a lion."

God shield us!—A lion among ladies is a most dreadful thing; for there is not a more fearful wild-flow than your lion living.

—Shakespeare,
A Midsummer Night's Dream

Chapter 1

KATHERINE SAW HIM JUST AS SHE REACHED FOR THE GLASS of champagne. Hand frozen in midair, caught by the shocked intensity of his narrowed dark eyes, she was unable to look away until a waiter questioned, "Mademoiselle?"

Her fingers closed around the cool crystal glass as she turned away. But even then, though she didn't allow herself to look his way, she felt the terrible force of Rashid Ben Hasir's stare and knew without looking around that he had moved toward her.

"Miss Bishop? It is Miss Bishop, isn't it?"

Katherine's fingers tightened around the delicate stem of her glass before she turned.

"It's been a long time," he said. "Six years?"

"Seven."

She had forgotten how tall he was, how dark his eyes were. The close-cropped black hair had touches of

9

silver now and so did the moustache that he had not had before.

"What are you doing in Rabat?" The voice that challenged her was the same as she remembered.

"I work here at the embassy. I'm assistant to the vice-consul."

"Oh?" Thick brows drew together in a scowl. "How long have you been here?"

"Three months."

"Have you seen Jamal?"

"Not yet." Katherine allowed herself a small smile. "Is he here in Rabat?"

"Occasionally. He spends most of his time either in Tangier or Marrakesh. Our family has business interests in both cities." He hesitated. "Does he know you're in Morocco?"

"No. I thought I'd wait until I settled in before I got in touch with him. It's been a long time. Perhaps he's forgotten me."

"I doubt that." His dark eyes raked her. "You've changed."

"Have I?"

"You wore sweaters and trousers. And you had your hair in a . . . how do you say? . . . a horse's tail?"

"Pony tail." She didn't smile.

"I like it better this way. You look quite elegant."

"Really?" Katherine's voice mocked him as she thought back to how she'd looked seven years ago. She'd still been awkward then, sure that she was too tall and too thin, wearing bulky sweaters to make herself look heavier and low heels to make herself look shorter. But the years had added self-confidence. She bought her clothes in Madrid or Casablanca now and wore high heels with ease. She knew that she looked good tonight in the white cashmere dress that flattered her slender figure and went well with the simplicity of her hairstyle. She still wore her wheat-blond hair long and straight, but tonight, as on most formal occasions, she'd drawn it back from her face and twisted it into a chignon at the nape of her neck. Gold filigree earrings and necklace added to her white and gold look, a startling contrast to Rashid's handsome darkness and his soft gray djellaba, a long robe of fine gabardine.

He was handsome, Katherine realized with a shock. He stood a head taller than the other men in the room and it was obvious from the envious stares of the women around her that they found him attractive.

He wasn't as good-looking as his younger brother, of course. There was none of Jamal's gentleness in Rashid's rock-hard face. He looked as ruthless as Katherine knew from experience he was. His toughness showed in the hard line of his jaw and the piercing depths of his eyes.

She took a sip of her champagne, trying to think of some way to escape. But before she could move away she heard someone call, "Rashid!" and turned to see her boss, Wade Contney, hurrying toward them.

"I hoped you'd be here tonight," Contney said as he shook Rashid's hand. "Have you met Katherine? Kathy, this is Rashid Ben Hasir, under-secretary of the interior of Morocco."

"We've met." Her voice was coolly polite.

"Oh, where?"

"I met Miss Bishop several years ago when Jamal was at Princeton. He and Miss Bishop were . . ." The hesitation was almost imperceptible. "Friends," he finished.

"Leave it to that young brother of yours to find the prettiest girl in New Jersey. I've been half tempted to make Kathy wear a veil and bind up that hair of hers when she goes out on the street. But I don't suppose anything would disguise those yellow eyes."

"Yellow? You're mistaken, Wade. Miss Bishop's eyes are golden."

"Yellow or gold, it wouldn't surprise me if one of these days some hot-blooded Arab carries her off into the desert." Wade winked at Katherine. "Be careful of old friends wearing gray djellabas, Kathy." Then he slapped Rashid on the back and said, "Since you two are old friends you can be dinner partners. After dinner we're going to the casino. I hope you'll be Kathy's escort, Rashid."

"Of course. Nothing would give me greater pleasure." His lips curved in a smile that didn't quite reach his eyes.

God, how she hated him! How she wanted to say, Go to hell, Rashid Ben Hasir. I wouldn't sit next to you if I had two broken legs and you offered me the only chair in the room.

But she was trapped by protocol; she worked for the United States Embassy and Rashid was an official for the government of Morocco. Wade Contney liked her and depended on her, but he was a career diplomat. If she stepped out of line and insulted a man in Rashid's position he'd send her packing.

"Come along," Wade said, motioning to the guests that it was time to go to dinner.

Katherine tried not to flinch when Rashid put his

hand on her bare arm, his black eyes mocking when he said, "Shall we, Miss Bishop?" Then leaning close he whispered, "Don't look so angry. Your boss is watching."

"You haven't changed, have you?" she said in a silken voice. "You're still telling people what to do. Do you still tell Jamal what to do?"

Dark eyes narrowed as he pulled her chair out and helped seat her. "Only when I think it's necessary," he murmured. "Do you really intend to see him while you're here?"

"Of course. I plan to take up just where we left off seven years ago."

Rashid's mouth tightened with anger, but before he could speak Katherine turned to the man on her right and began to chat, feeling a malicious satisfaction when she saw that Rashid had been trapped into a one-sided conversation with the blue-haired wife of a German industrialist.

On the outside the Casino de Rabat was a beautiful, well-lit building. The inside, however, was a huge Arab tent draped in red and gold brocade. The lighting was dim, each table illuminated only by candles in tall brass candlesticks. The tables were knee-high, the chairs and divans low and plush. The faint scent of incense permeated the air.

Because Katherine had made sure the other guests had proper transportation and were safely on their way before she left, she and Rashid were the last to arrive at the casino. The other members of the party were already seated at one large round table.

"I'm sorry," the waiter apologized to Rashid. "But

there was an error. I'm afraid there is no room for you and the young lady with your party. But if you don't mind I have a nice table near the dance floor."

The suggestion of a smile curved Rashid's mouth. "That's quite all right," he said, his hand tightening on Katherine's arm as they followed the waiter to a low red divan in a dimly lit alcove. "This will do nicely, thank you. Will you bring us a bottle of champagne, please? Dom Perignon '79, if you have it."

"Oui, Monsieur. *Très bien."*

Katherine settled back on the built-for-two sofa, trying to see the table where Wade Contney and the rest of the party were seated. "The least the waiter could have done is to have given us a table within shouting distance of the others," she murmured.

"Do you think you need to shout?"

Biting her lip in annoyance, Katherine shot him an angry look. "I think we'd both be more comfortable with other people. After all, I doubt that we have very much to talk about."

"Oh, I don't know. We can talk about Princeton, about you, your studies. What have you done with yourself since the last time I saw you? You had one more year at school, didn't you?"

"Yes." She tapped her fingers impatiently, then said, "But I quit school for a year."

"Quit? But why?"

"For fun," she snapped. "I thought it would be fun just to laze around for a year."

"I see. And after school?"

"The State Department. I started as a junior secretary in Washington. I managed to get my master's degree there too. Then after Washington I went to

Mexico City. Wade worked there, and when he was transferred here he requested me."

A waiter arrived, and after the champagne had been opened and tasted Rashid motioned the man away. He poured a glass and handed it to Katherine. Then he filled his own and, looking over the rim of it, said, "Have you and Jamal kept in touch these past seven years?"

"No."

"Do you think it's a good idea to see him now? It's been a long time; you've both changed and—"

"Here you are!" Wade Contney boomed as he reached their table. "Darn shame you're not with us. I raised hell with the head waiter." He grinned at Rashid. "But I can think of a lot worse things than being in a secluded corner with a beautiful woman like Kathy. You two have yourselves a fine evening. Incidentally, Kathy, I told Herr Gutterman you'd see to his problem personally tomorrow morning. I know he's a royal pain, but he likes you and you seem to know how to deal with him. I told him ten o'clock. All right?"

Her frown was barely noticeable. "Of course, Wade."

When Contney turned away Rashid said, "You don't like Gutterman?"

"Not particularly."

"Why?"

"He doesn't know how to keep his hands to himself."

"Then you shouldn't have to deal with him."

"I have to deal with a lot of people I don't like." Her voice was cool. "It's part of my job."

"Like tonight?"

Katherine shrugged, looking away from him as a five-piece band began to play. The instruments, typically Moroccan, consisted of a kanaine, which was similar to a zither, a long bamboo flute, a tambourine and two drums. The music, almost oriental in its flavor, rose to a high pitch as a dancer whirled onto the stage, a tray with glasses of water on his head. Around and around the dancer whirled, finally ending the dance flat on his stomach, his head held high, with all the water glasses safely intact.

He was followed by a snake charmer. Katherine, who had always been terrified of snakes, tried to quell her fear when a cobra, no more than six feet from her, coiled, then raised his flat head and began to sway to the high thin wail of the snake charmer's flute.

As hypnotized as the cobra, she wasn't even aware that she moved closer to Rashid or that his arm curved the back of her seat. She gave a sigh of relief when the music turned from sinister to sensual and the snake charmer left and a dancer, clad in multitudinous layers of pink chiffon, ran onto the stage. One by one, in time to the music, the veils were tossed aside until the woman was clad only in a few swathes of pink.

The music became more provocative as she gyrated, her stomach rolling, her hips moving. Silver-belled bracelets worn around her wrists and ankles jingled in time to the music. Her long delicate fingers sent a come-to-me message; her long black hair swirled around her body as she twisted her ample curves.

Katherine glanced around her, studying the faces of the men seated nearby. Their eyes were intent on the dancer as they leaned forward. She could almost feel their excitement, their barely suppressed desire for the woman. When the dance ended in a crescendo of music, the dancer supine on the floor, her body heaving with an imitation of passion that seemed more like exhaustion to Katherine, Rashid turned to her and asked, "Well, what do you think of our famous belly dance?"

"Interesting." She took a slow sip of the champagne. "And amusing."

One eyebrow cocked in question. "Amusing?"

"I find it amusing that in a country where you keep your women covered from the tops of their heads to their toes that you men can get such lascivious pleasure from watching a rather plump woman dance."

"Plump?"

"She was at least twenty pounds overweight."

"Ah, but you see we Moroccans don't have the fetish about weight that you Americans have. We like our women with a little meat on their bones."

"How fortunate then that they wear long robes." She felt a little curl of pleasure at the sudden narrowing of his eyes.

They didn't speak for several long moments. Then finally Rashid said, "There are many differences in our cultures, Katherine. The fact that our women are covered and veiled is only one of them. We think differently than you do. We worship different gods. And although things are changing here there are many who prefer the old ways. There are women who prefer to be veiled, and even if they didn't, their husbands would insist on it."

"That doesn't surprise me. I'm sure the men like things just the way they are."

"Naturally." His lips curved in a mocking smile.

"Why would we want to change what is already perfect?" Then, before she could reply, he said, "Why do you want to see my brother?"

"We were good friends—until you came, of course."

"I only did what I thought was best for both of you at the time. You were too young to know what you wanted, too young to make such a serious step as marriage."

She could feel the anger begin to build, feel the need to strike out against the remembered hurt. Trying to control herself she glanced at her watch and said, "I have that appointment with Herr Gutterman at ten in the morning and there are things I have to do before that. I really must leave now. Please don't bother seeing me home. There are taxis just outside."

"Nonsense. Of course I'll take you home."

He looked around for the waiter who—like waiters all over the world—seemed to disappear the minute Rashid tried to get his attention. In the meantime, a different orchestra had begun to play European music.

"We might as well have a dance while we're waiting," Rashid said. Before Katherine could object he took her arm and led her out onto the dance floor. When he pulled her into his arms she knew he could feel the stiffness of her body. That was all right, she thought, she wanted him to know that she didn't want to be here with him, didn't want his arms around her.

A woman stepped to the microphone and in a sensuously throaty voice began to sing a medley of French songs. As "Under Paris Skies" segued into "C'est Si Bon" and "April in Paris," couples moved slower. It seemed to Katherine as though they were all enfolded in the blue haze of smoke that hung like a veil over the tented room. She could smell the incense, and mingled with it the scent of Rashid's sandalwood after-shave as he pulled her closer.

They danced well together. Half a foot taller than she, he held her against his muscled body, his hand firm and warm against her back.

When she felt her breath quicken and a strange dryness in her mouth, Katherine tried to move away. But his fingers curled around hers and the hand against her back held her tightly against him. They moved to the romantic rhythm of "La Vie en Rose," the hauntingly beautiful song that seemed to express all of the romance that was Paris. And at last Katherine closed her eyes and gave herself up to the music. In a little while it seemed as though everything else had been shut out. There was only the music, the throaty voice of the woman singing and the feel of Rashid's shoulder against her cheek. That's all there was and that's all that mattered. She felt suspended, she and this man, alone in the dimly lit tent, moving slowly together, bodies close and touching.

His hand tightened on hers and she felt the brush of his lips against her hair. She tried to move away and could not because she was held, held by the music and by him and by a strange longing that kept her, for just this small space of time, a willing captive.

When the music stopped he still held her locked in his embrace. Hot color crept to Katherine's cheeks as her eyes met his. She saw the flare of his nostrils and felt herself sway toward him. For a moment his hands tightened on her arms and he seemed about to speak.

Abruptly he let her go and led her off the dance floor. He signaled for the waiter and when Katherine said, "I can get a cab. Why don't you join the others?" he answered, "Nonsense," and slapped a handful of dirhams onto the table.

They didn't speak until they were in the silver-gray Mercedes coupe. "Where do you live?" he asked.

"On El Jadida. Number twenty-five."

They drove through the now quiet streets without speaking. When they reached her street she said, "Near the end of the block. The building on the right."

When Rashid stopped in front of the apartment he switched off the motor and said, "I'll walk you to your door."

"That's not necessary."

"Please wait," he snapped, then got out and walked around the car to help her out. With his hand still holding hers he looked down at her. "Jamal will be here on business next week," he said. "I'll tell him you're at the embassy."

"Thank you, Rashid." She pulled her hand away.

But he turned and with his hand on her arm led her into the building. "Where is your apartment?" he asked.

"Upstairs, but—"

He let her precede him up the stairs. When she stopped in front of the door he put his hand out for her key and as he opened the door he said, "Good night. Thank you for a most interesting evening."

Her face tightened. "Thank you for bringing me home."

She turned to go in and when she did he put his

hand on her arm. "I want to tell you something, Katherine. I want you to know that there was nothing personal when I separated you and Jamal. You were both too young to really know what you wanted. I did what I thought was best for both of you."

"And now?" She challenged him. "Are Jamal and I old enough now, Rashid? Or are you still playing big brother? Are you still trying to live Jamal's life for him?"

"You don't understand, do you?" He gripped her arms, forcing her to face him. "It's not that I object to you. It's a question of different cultures, of—"

"Let me go!" Katherine tried to pull away from him but his grip on her arms tightened. "Damn you," she said, "let me go."

His face was white with anger as he glared down at her. Then, before she could escape his grasp, he pulled her to him and his angry mouth descended on hers in a kiss so fierce she felt her breath catch.

His lips ground against her and his tongue probed her lips, trying to force them apart. When she resisted he nipped her bottom lip and when she gasped his tongue, like a warm shaft of fire, invaded her mouth. Fingers like steel dug into her shoulders, but when she gave a small whimper of pain his hands loosened their grip. He still held her but he didn't hurt her. He caught the lip he had injured between his strong white teeth and caressed it with the tip of his tongue. Then he kissed her again, his lips warm against hers.

Katherine felt herself sway toward him, felt a traitorous heat creep through her body. She tried to pull away but the hands on her shoulders tightened again.

Then, almost as abruptly as he had taken her, he let her go. "I'm sorry," he said in a hoarse voice. He looked down at her with smoldering eyes. "I didn't mean to do that. You made me angry. I'm sorry."

Before she could reply he turned on his heel and moved quickly down the broad winding stairs.

Chapter 2

KATHERINE STOOD OUTSIDE HER DOOR UNTIL SHE HEARD the downstairs door slam shut, the low growl of the Mercedes and the screech of tires as Rashid pulled away. When she went in she closed her door and stood there in the darkness, trembling with reaction. Remembering, remembering how it had been that year at Princeton.

"He's a hunk! Dark soulful eyes, full sexy lips, the best-looking buns on campus." Annie McAllister's eyes sparkled with fun. "Come on, Kathy, he's dying to meet you."

Katherine shook her head. *"Merci, gracias, danke.* Thanks but no thanks. I know what your blind dates are like."

"They haven't been all bad," Annie protested.

"Let me see, there was Dave what's-his-name, the

23

psych major. You said he was a great dancer but you neglected to tell me he was only five feet tall.''

"He wasn't that short," Annie said with a grin.

"Then why did he dance with his nose in my navel? And what about that guy you play tennis with? Jack-the-zipper? He nearly tore my new blouse off.''

"You've got great bazooms, kid. You can't blame him for trying." Annie closed the book she'd been studying and stood up to flex her shoulders. "Jamal is different, Kathy. He's one of the best-looking men I've ever seen.''

"Jamal? What kind of a name is that?"

"Moroccan. He's from Marrakesh. I met him last weekend at Pete's fraternity party. Half the girls there went cross-eyed when they saw him. He's gorgeous.''

"Then why can't he get his own date?"

"He's got more dates than he can handle, Kathy. But he saw you at the game Saturday and wants to meet you. Come on, be a sport. The guy's okay. He's handsome, sexy and he's got a red Corvette. What more do you want? We're going to a Grieg concert tomorrow night. What can happen? I promise we won't split up. I'll stick close till we get back here.''

"You promise?"

"Absolutely."

Annie's "absolutely" meant until halfway through the concert. At the intermission she said, "Pete and I are going to split. If I hear one more song in Norwegian my ears'll drop off." Before Katherine could object Annie grabbed Pete's arm, waggled her fingers and dashed away.

Jamal Ben Hasir raised his dark brows and said, "I'm

rather enjoying the concert, but if you'd like to leave I'll be happy to see you back to your dormitory."

Katherine studied him, then after a moment's hesitation said, "No, let's stay," and allowed him to take her arm and lead her back to their seats.

She had to admit that Jamal was a cut above the other blind dates Annie had arranged. He was twenty-one, a year older than she, and taller by a good six inches. His skin was a golden tan, his hair thick and black. He had classically even features and his wide brown eyes were as soulful as Annie had said they were. He was polite and—unless it was a very good act—he was as shy as Katherine.

But her guard was still up when they left the auditorium to walk back to her dorm. It had started to snow while they were at the concert. The ground was white in the moonlight and the trees hung heavy with crystal icicles. When she looked up at Jamal she saw snow-flakes on his long dark eyelashes and thought, Annie's right, he's gorgeous.

He shook hands with her when they reached her dorm. The next day he sent her two dozen yellow roses with a card reading, "Thank you for a most enjoyable evening. May I see you Saturday night for dinner?"

"Jeeze Louise," Nancy Perkins said, reading the card over her shoulder. "Kathy's hooked the Arab."

Katherine glowered at Nancy as she gathered the roses and stomped up to her room. But she was smiling when she closed the door.

Saturday night Jamal took her to one of Princeton's plushest restaurants. He was attentive and charming and didn't try to kiss her. The next day she received an elaborately wrapped gift box and inside was a stuffed animal, a sad-eyed basset she promptly named Bruce.

The dates continued. She insisted that he not send any more gifts and he said, "But Kathy, these are just little things to show you how much I like being with you."

Who could resist a four-foot giraffe, a nosegay of violets, a box of imported chocolates? For the first time in her life Katherine felt pampered. It was a delicious feeling. She liked Jamal—what girl in her right mind wouldn't? He was handsome, generous, attentive and fascinatingly foreign. This was his second year at Princeton. He'd leave in June to go back to his own country and finish his education there. His father was dead. He had a brother who was eight years older and a grandfather who lived in Marrakesh. His grandmother lived in Paris.

"In Paris?" Katherine was surprised. "Is she French?"

"Very French." Jamal smiled. "Too French to live with my grandfather, apparently. They've been separated for thirteen years."

"But never divorced?"

"No. And that's strange because divorce isn't all that difficult in my country. Everyone expected Granddad to divorce Grandmother when she left him. Or even to marry again without benefit of divorce."

"Can a man do that? Marry without divorcing, I mean?"

"In my country a man can have four wives."

"Four wives! That's awful!"

"Not so awful—at least not for the man." Jamal laughed. "As long as he can afford them. All of his wives must have separate houses, of course, and they should all be treated equally. If he buys a new robe for one then he must buy a new robe for all. It works out quite well."

"Did *your* father have four wives?"

"Only two."

"Do they get along?"

"My mother died when I was two, Katherine. Rashid's mother died last year. But yes, I suppose they got along."

Katherine stared at him in disbelief. "Incredible," she murmured. "Absolutely incredible."

"Customs, my dear Kathy. You think it's incredible but we see nothing unusual about it. You must remember though that not every man in Morocco has four wives. I'd guess that perhaps only one in two hundred has more than one wife because not too many can afford to keep four women. Also, for many men one woman is enough for a lifetime."

"I'm glad to hear *that.*"

Impulsively Jamal hugged her. "You're so sweet, Kathy, and so naive that you make me want to protect you."

"Jamal . . ."

"I like your shyness, your quietness and your reserve. I like the way the sun turns your hair to gold. I like . . ."

He kissed her, gently and sweetly, and she melted into his arms.

With that kiss their relationship began to change. The gentle good-night kisses became more passionate. Jamal was persistently ardent but he never went further than Katherine permitted him to go. Nor did he get angry like the other young men she'd rebuffed, young men who stomped off in a rage when she'd asked them to stop.

Jamal would only sigh and say, in a sadly agonized voice, "You're going to drive me crazy." But he never got angry and he never stomped off.

Katherine adored him.

That Christmas she took him home to Maine to meet her parents. When she told them on the phone she wanted to bring a friend along her father said, "An *A*-rab?" But once he met Jamal there'd been no problems. He asked endless questions about Morocco and found it fascinating that men there were allowed four wives. Her mother had been less than charmed by the idea, but softened on Christmas morning when she opened her gifts to find a green and gold brocade caftan.

"It's only a small thank-you for allowing me to come into your home," Jamal said with a smile. "There are times when I miss my own family and it's—what do you say?—it's warming to be included in your festivities."

"He's a nice boy," her father told her that night after Jamal had gone to the guest room. "A real gentleman, anybody can see that. But I can't say as I'd like to see you too interested in a fella who might end up having a whole bunch of wives."

"He explained that to me, Dad. He said that maybe only one man in two hundred has more than one. Anyway, Jamal and I are only friends."

"You're not serious about him then?"

"No Dad, we're just friends. Really."

That wasn't quite true, of course. Katherine liked Jamal a lot more than she wanted to admit, more than any man she'd ever dated. Heaven knows she felt yearnings she'd never felt before. It was becoming more and more difficult to push Jamal away on some of those moonlit nights when they parked in his Corvette. With his arms around her and his mouth so warm and urgent against hers, it was hard to remember the stern admonishments of her parents and her own high standards.

Katherine had never been a popular girl and it was exciting to have a man as handsome and nice as Jamal pay attention to her. The tallest girl in her class at high school, Katherine had felt awkward and painfully shy. She didn't want to be five foot eight, she wanted to be five foot two. Over her mother's pained objections she had insisted on wearing frilly dresses designed for shorter girls, dresses that looked terrible on her. She had also insisted on wearing her fine wheat-gold hair frizzed into tight little curls. By the time she got to college she was able to accept her height and leave the frills and frizzies behind in Maine. But she still felt shy and awkward.

Small, dark-haired Annie McAllister, who had been her roommate since freshman year, had been so obviously admiring of Katherine's looks that slowly but surely she gained some measure of self-confidence.

When Jamal, who obviously could have had his pick of any girl on campus, came into Katherine's life, her self-esteem rose another ten points.

They continued to see each other all that winter. Jamal would leave in June but Katherine had another year of school. It had been a struggle for her parents to send her to Princeton, even with her partial scholarship, and she'd worked every summer to help. But the last year had been difficult for her father and she was not too surprised when, in February, she received an apologetic letter from him saying he just didn't know how he could manage to scrape up enough money for her final year.

Katherine was tight-lipped with worry for a week. Then she wrote her father to say that it really was all right, she needed a year off to clear her mind and think things over. She'd work for a year, living at home to save money if that was all right with him and her mother, then finish her studies at the University of Maine.

She didn't tell Jamal or Annie what her plans were. There would be time enough for that later.

Winter snows finally gave way to spring rains. Buds swelled into flowering blossoms and the sweet scent of promise filled the air. It was a flowering time, a time for young lovers. One night as they walked slowly back along the path leading to Katherine's dormitory, Jamal suddenly stopped and pulled her into his arms.

"I love you," he whispered. "Please, Kathy, love me too."

"I do," she said in a trembling voice. "Oh, Jamal, I do, but . . ."

"But what?"

"You're going back to Morocco and I haven't finished school yet."

"Forget school. Come back to Morocco with me."

"I can't do that."

"Of course you can. We'll be married before I leave."

When she still hesitated he hugged her. "I love you, Kathy, and I want to be with you. I can't stand leaving you every night like this." He smoothed the fair hair back from her face and tenderly kissed her eyelids. "I want you so," he whispered. "Please, darling, say yes."

"Yes, Jamal," she said. "Yes, I'll marry you."

She telephoned her parents the next day. Her mother, after first bursting into tears, said, "A June wedding! Darling, how wonderful. We'll have to paint the living room and dining room, of course. And fix the front porch. I've been after your father for the last ten years to do the porch. And we'll have to reserve the church. You know how busy St. Stevens is in June. Mamie Schofield's daughter is getting married on the tenth, so that day's taken, but—"

"Mama," Katherine broke in with a laugh. "Calm down, Mama. We haven't even set the date yet."

"But you will be married here in Buckport?"

"Yes, of course. But I only said yes last night. We haven't had time to make any plans."

"You'll let me know though? As soon as you know something you'll let me know? Oh, darling, I'm so happy for you."

Her father, however, didn't share her mother's enthusiasm. He had little to say on the phone, but he wrote her a long letter cautioning her to think things over. There was a difference in religion, he warned, as well as in customs. How could she live in a country where women were veiled and men were allowed to have four wives?

"Would I have to wear a veil?" she asked Jamal.

"No, of course not, at least not most of the time." He kissed the tip of her nose. "Don't worry, Kathy, as long as we love each other everything will be all right."

Life had never been so wonderful for Katherine. She

was twenty years old and in love. She knew exactly what she was going to do with her life. Everything was lovely; nothing could happen to mar her happiness.

But something did happen, of course, and that something was Rashid.

For days that long-ago spring Jamal talked of nothing else except his older brother's impending visit. Rashid had written that he planned to attend the Princeton reunion in June and Jamal was beside himself with excitement.

"I can't wait to have him meet you," he told Katherine.

"Have you told him about us?"

"Of course. I wrote him about you the first night we met."

"Does he know we're engaged?"

He nodded. "That's probably why he decided to come."

"I wish you hadn't told him."

"Not tell Rashid? You don't understand, Kathy. Rashid is more than my older brother. He helped raise me—I've always depended on him. He's always been there for me when I needed him." He laughed and hugged her. "Don't look so worried, darling. Rashid is going to be crazy about you."

Despite his reassuring words, Katherine felt a small nudge of fear. A fear she knew was justified the minute she saw Rashid Ben Hasir at the Friday night cocktail party marking the beginning of the reunion. Most of the men were dressed in blue jeans and class T-shirts. There were a few sport shirts and blazers, even one or two cowboy hats and several casual summer suits.

Rashid, dressed in an obviously expensive dark blue suit, crisp white shirt and dark tie, seemed out of place with the blue-jeaned young men and even with the older alumni.

He was taller than Jamal and of a broader build. Although it was possible to tell they were brothers, his face had none of the softness of Jamal's. His eyes had a coldly speculative look that made him appear older than twenty-nine. She found his mouth cruel-looking, but strangely sensuous as well.

He was polite, of course, but for the first time in a long time Katherine felt the same too-tall awkwardness she'd felt in high school. After they were introduced she thrust her damp hands into the pockets of her new hunter-green jacket, swallowed nervously and managed to ask how it felt to be back at Princeton.

Rashid's reply was coolly pleasant. He remained coolly pleasant all that weekend. The three of them went to a rugby game the next day and that night he took Katherine and Jamal into New York for dinner at 21.

She didn't see Jamal on Sunday. The campus was still a buzz of activity but she stayed in the dorm waiting for his call. She told herself the two brothers had a lot to talk about and there was no reason to be worried.

Jamal didn't call on Monday or Tuesday. On Wednesday Rashid phoned to invite her to dinner.

"The Harbor House at eight?" he asked.

"Yes, thank you, that will be fine."

"Take a taxi. I'll wait for you at the entrance."

I'll wait for you at the entrance? Katherine's hand tightened around the telephone, but before she could ask about Jamal, Rashid hung up.

That night she and Annie rummaged through her closet, inspecting and rejecting almost everything in it. Finally the choice of what to wear narrowed down to a three-year-old navy-blue suit and a lightweight wool dress.

"It's too warm for the wool," Annie said, "but wear it anyway. It's the best thing you have and it looks great with your complexion and hair. You can borrow my gold loop earrings and my gold belt."

By seven-thirty, looking much better than she felt, Katherine was ready. Annie had been right, the beige dress looked good on her. She'd washed her wheat-colored hair, and at Annie's insistence let it hang free around her shoulders. Also at Annie's insistence she wore her only pair of two-inch heels.

"I look like a giant," she moaned.

"Don't be a sap. Both Jamal and his brother are over six feet. You look beautiful. Jamal has probably told Rashid that he wants to marry you and tonight is family-blessing night. Relax."

"Relax, relax," Katherine told herself all the way in the taxi. But she couldn't. She was nervous and tense and hot. She dabbed at the perspiration beading her upper lip but when the driver asked if she wanted the windows open she said no because she didn't want her hair to blow.

Please let Jamal be there, she prayed.

But he wasn't there. When the taxi pulled up to the curb it was Rashid who stepped forward to open the door and help her out. Then he paid for the taxi and led her into the restaurant.

"Is Jamal here?" she asked, trying to see in the dim light.

"No."

"Will he be coming later?"

Rashid took her arm and followed the maitre d' to a secluded table. When she was seated he said, "Jamal isn't coming, Katherine."

"I see." She didn't, of course. Why would Rashid want to be alone with her? Why hadn't Jamal called? Where was Jamal?

"Would you like a drink?"

"A glass of white wine, please."

He motioned for the waiter. "A glass of white wine for the young lady and a martini on the rocks for me." When the man turned away Rashid said, "Moslems don't drink, you know. It's against our religion. But I have to confess to a special liking for martinis. I allow myself one occasionally, on very special or very trying occasions."

"Which is this?" Katherine tightened her hands together in her lap.

"Both, I think. Ah, here we are. Shall we drink to Princeton?"

"Of course." Her hand shook when she picked up the glass. "What was your major?"

"Economics. What about you? What is your major?"

"French, with a minor in political science. I'm not sure yet what I want to do."

"Why not try for the State Department? If you're good at languages and interested in political science it seems to me you could tie them together. Too many diplomats don't even make an attempt to learn the language of the country they're in. It's a mistake, of course. How can they hope to communicate with people they can't talk to?"

With great ease he carried the conversation while Katherine sipped her wine and knew he hadn't invited her here to talk about their majors and minors or diplomacy. When their dinner came she nibbled at her salmon while he ate his shishkabob.

Finally, halfway through the meal, he said, "I know you're wondering why I wanted to talk to you, Katherine."

She looked at him across the table.

"It's about you and Jamal, of course."

She took a deep breath and put her fork down. "Of course."

"You're both very young. You're what? Nineteen?"

"I'm twenty."

"Much too young to consider a serious step like marriage, especially if you want to finish your education."

"I could go to school in Morocco."

"Perhaps. But once you and Jamal start having children that would be out of the question." He shook his head and in a patient voice said, "It would be better for both of you if you waited two or three years."

"How . . . how does Jamal feel about that?"

"He's seen the logic of it. If you're still in love two or three years from now we can talk about this again."

"We can talk about this again!" Her whole body tensed in anger. "This is between Jamal and me. It has nothing to do with you."

The dark eyes narrowed. "I'm Jamal's guardian until he's twenty-five. He'll do what I tell him to do. Marriage at this time in his life is out of the question."

"Especially to an American?"

"That's right. Especially to an American who is a Christian."

"Where is Jamal?"

"I put him on a plane for Casablanca this morning."

Katherine stared at him, unable for a moment to comprehend the words. Jamal wouldn't leave, not without telling her.

"I'm sorry," Rashid went on. "We thought it was best."

"We thought it best! *You* thought it best, so you've stepped in and turned our lives around." She slapped her napkin down on the table and pushed her chair back.

"Please don't leave," Rashid said. "I haven't finished."

"Well I have." But before she could move his hand clamped on her wrist and he said, "Don't make a scene. I have something else to say to you."

"I don't want to hear anything you have to say." Katherine tried to rise but the hand on her wrist tightened. The sensuously cruel mouth thinned. "Wait until I've finished," he warned. "Then I'll put you in a cab."

There was nothing Katherine could do if she didn't want to make a scene, and diners were already turning to look at them curiously.

"That's better," Rashid said and the pressure on her arm eased. "I've made inquiries about you. It seems that you're an exceptionally bright girl and a good student. When you graduate next year you plan to go on and get a master's degree. That's admirable. I understand you're upset and you can't see—at least

right now—that this is for your own good. In a few
months you'll forget about Jamal and get on with your
life. However, to compensate for any pain that Jamal's
leaving has caused, and to help a bit with your education, I'd like you to take this."

He reached into his breast pocket and, withdrawing a
check, handed it to her. When she didn't take it he said,
"It's for twenty thousand dollars, Katherine."

"Twenty thousand dollars!" Almost without thinking
she reached for the check and looked at it. "Twenty
thousand dollars," she said again.

"Toward your education." There was a note of irony
in his voice. "And to help ease the pain of losing Jamal,
of course."

Katherine looked from him to the check and felt the
sickness of rage rising in her throat. "How dare you?"
she whispered. "How dare you?"

"Oh come now. There's no need to be dramatic."
His smile was condescending, superior. "You've played
your little scene of pretending to be insulted. Now take
the money and enjoy it."

"Enjoy it?" She shoved her chair back from the
table, not even aware that her voice had risen or that
she was crying and that people were staring. "You take
your money," she shouted between sobs. "Take it and
stick it . . . stick it on your shishkabob!" Then before
he could stop her she ripped the check in two and flung
it on the table and ran out of the restaurant.

She had not seen Rashid Ben Hasir again—until
tonight. For seven long years she had thought about
him. And she had known that someday, somehow, she
would make him sorry for what he had done to her.

Chapter 3

"IT'S A MIRACLE," JAMAL SAID WHEN HE CALLED HER. "I can't believe you're here. When can I see you? Are you free for dinner tonight?"

"Sorry, I have plans." Her words were restrained and cool.

"Then tomorrow. Please, Kathy, I'm dying to see you. Eight o'clock?"

Katherine hesitated, then finally said, "Yes, all right. Eight is fine."

When she put the phone down she was surprised to see that her hands were shaking. She'd thought about Jamal for seven years. Now that she was going to see him all the old hurt and anger came rushing back. For a long time she had tried to tell herself that Jamal had been too immature to stand up to a man as strong-willed as Rashid. But she'd been shaken by his weakness and by what she believed to be an act of

cowardice. She hadn't answered the letter he wrote
begging her forgiveness, nor any of the letters that
followed.

Now they were both here in Rabat and tomorrow she
would see him.

The next night Katherine chose a sea-green silk dress
that did nice things for her figure. She twisted her long
blond hair into a chignon at the nape of her slender
neck and clipped a jade butterfly to one side of it. For
jewelry she wore a gold sanddollar necklace with
matching earrings.

She tensed when the buzzer rang, then, drawing a
deep breath to steady herself, she opened the door.

The boy had become a devastatingly handsome man.

"Hello, Jamal," she said. "How nice to see you
again."

White teeth caught his lower lip as he looked at her.
Then he smiled an apologetic smile and said, "Hello,
Kathy."

"Come in."

"Thank you." He glanced around the apartment.
"This is nice."

"I've only been here a few months. It needs a bit of
fixing up, a painting or two, some personal touches.
Would you like a drink?"

"Perrier if you have it."

"Yes, of course." She went to prepare the drinks:
Perrier for him, a gin and tonic for herself. When she
returned she sat across from him on the lemon-yellow
sofa.

"I can't believe you're really here in Morocco," he
said in a low voice. "It's been a long time."

Half-forgotten feelings stirred. "Yes, a long time."

He looked at her over the rim of his glass. "Here's to old acquaintance, Kathy."

"To old acquaintance."

"Have you ever forgiven me for leaving?"

"I'm not sure."

"I couldn't help it."

"Couldn't you?"

"Rashid made me leave. There wasn't anything I could do." His dark eyes looked beseechingly into hers. "He said he'd never allow the marriage, that I was too young, that a marriage between a Christian and a Moslem wouldn't work. I didn't know what to do. I was only twenty-one and Rashid . . . Rashid was so damned forceful. He packed my bags and put me on a plane for Casablanca. There wasn't anything I could do about it."

"You could have called me."

"He said that it would be easier for you if I didn't. He said that he'd take care of everything." Jamal put his drink down and came to sit beside her on the sofa. "I'm so sorry," he said as he took her hand. "Forgive me, Kathy. Give me a chance to make it up to you."

Katherine hesitated and in a careful voice said, "I suppose there isn't any reason why we can't be friends."

"Friends? I want us to be more than friends, Kathy. I want it to be like it was seven years ago."

"Jamal—"

"No, don't say anything now. I know I'm rushing things but I want you to know that nothing has changed. You were my first love, Kathy. I was a fool to leave you." His lips brushed hers. "Now how about dinner? Have you been to the Rif?"

Katherine shook her head, almost too breathless to speak.

"Have you gotten accustomed to Moroccan food?"

"Yes, I love it."

"Good. The Rif has some of the best food in Rabat."

The restaurant, dimly lit with ornate golden lamps and candelabra, was plushly elegant. The rich carpets for which Rabat is famed were scattered over tiled floors. Carved Moorish arches separated different sections of the room to give the diners more privacy.

"A champagne cocktail for mademoiselle," Jamal said when they were seated. "*Sidi* Harazem for me."

He was amusing and charming and in spite of Katherine's initial reserve she found herself relaxing. When she commented on the restaurant Jamal said, "Tomorrow night we'll try the Koutoubia. Their bastilla—you know what that is, don't you? pigeon stuffed with almonds—is fantastic. Saturday we'll go to the casino. Perhaps Sunday you'd like to drive into Casablanca for dinner and a show."

"Slow down, Jamal," Katherine said with a smile. "You're trying to sweep me off my feet."

"Off of your feet right into my arms." He leaned to kiss her cheek and when he put his arm around her she moved closer. They sat like that, without speaking, until the waiter began to serve them.

The harira soup was served with delicate slices of lemon. That was followed by couscous, steamed semolina with tender mutton and vegetables cooked to perfection.

"Sweet agony," Katherine said when the waiter finally took away the dishes and placed a glass of hot mint tea in front of her. She smiled at Jamal and felt the earlier tension slide away. When he reached for her hand she gave it willingly. And when, on the drive to her apartment, he pulled her over close to him she rested her head on his shoulder, remembering Princeton and the red Corvette and the way it had been.

He didn't ask to come in. "I'll pick you up tomorrow night," he said. "We'll have dinner and go dancing."

Katherine looked at him. She reached out and touched the side of his face. "Jamal, I don't know. I don't think we should rush this. We've been apart for a long time. We've both changed."

"The way we feel about each other hasn't changed, Kathy. All I'm asking for is a chance to make up for the seven years we've been apart."

Before she could object he pulled her into his arms and kissed her. It had been so long, she thought. She wanted to recapture the feelings she'd had that long-ago spring when she had been twenty. His lips were as sweetly tender as she remembered, his arms strong and young.

When he let her go he said, "You see, nothing has changed, has it?"

Katherine leaned her head against his shoulder. "No," she said, "nothing has changed."

And knew that she lied.

The next morning he sent her two dozen yellow roses.

She saw him three times that week before he had to return to Tangier on business. A week later he came back and they saw each other every night. He was gay

and charming and dear. She liked being with him and
tried not to admit to herself that something was missing.

It's natural, she thought. Seven years have passed.
We've changed. We're different people.

It had taken a long time after Jamal left for her to
even look at a man. She'd had no dates that first year
because she'd been working such long hours. But
finally, when she went back to school, she began to
date. She'd had several minor romances during the next
few years but she'd never been able to feel about a man
the way she'd felt about Jamal that year at Princeton.
He'd been her first love; he was difficult to forget.

Now he'd walked back into her life and she wasn't
sure how she felt about it. In some ways he hadn't
changed; he was still the boy she had known so long
ago. He still sent flowers and small gifts—a pair of
silver earrings, embroidered cocktail napkins, a soft
leather billfold, a slave bracelet that he insisted on
fastening around her ankle.

"There now," he said as he kissed her instep, "you're
my slave." He pretended to twirl a moustache he didn't
have. "A slave to my most fiendish passions, my every
whim, my wild desire." He nipped her ankle, then,
pushing her back against the yellow sofa began to tickle
her, then smother her with kisses. But suddenly her
closeness—the feel of her body, helpless with laughter
under his, the softness and the scent of her—was too
much.

His arms tightened around her as his mouth sought
hers. "Kathy," he whispered as he pulled her closer, his
body taut with longing.

"Jamal, don't . . ."

"Darling, please. Please." A hand closed on her breast. "Kathy, I love you. I want you. I—"

"No!" She pulled away from him. "No," she said again and sat up.

For a long time they didn't speak. Then he reached over and took her hand. "I don't blame you for the way you feel," he said in a low voice. "It's my fault because I left you. How can I expect you to believe in me again?" He brought her hand to his lips. "But I am going to make you believe in me again, Kathy. I am going to make you forget that I let Rashid separate us."

He didn't mention Rashid's name again until a week later. "Rashid's going to be in Rabat this weekend," he said, trying to keep his voice casual. "He's asked us to have dinner with him Saturday."

"Saturday? I'm afraid I can't, Jamal. There's an embassy cocktail party I have to go to."

"Then we'll eat later." He turned her around and, putting a finger under her chin, lifted her face. "He's my brother, sweetheart. He honestly thought he'd done the right thing when he separated us. It was a long time ago. Now I'd like the two of you to be friends."

In the end Katherine agreed. Jamal and Rashid could pick her up at the embassy at eight-thirty. By eight-fifteen, when she excused herself and went to the ladies room to check her makeup, she was so nervous her mouth was dry. She'd decided to wear her hair down tonight and now she wished she hadn't because it made her look too young, too vulnerable. She wore a coral-pink suit with a pale pink evening blouse that probably was too daringly cut in the front, and high-heeled pink pumps. She brushed her hair, dabbed a bit of powder on her flushed cheeks and wished with all her heart she were back in Buckport.

They had dinner at a small but quite elegant French restaurant. Rashid was polite but had little to say. Jamal tried valiantly to keep the conversation going.

"I have a great idea," he said just as they started on dessert. "Next weekend is your Easter week, isn't it, Kathy?"

She nodded. "I have four days off."

"Any plans?"

"No."

"What about you, Rashid?"

"None that I remember at the moment."

"Then why don't the three of us fly to Marrakesh?"

Katherine's eyes widened. She glanced at Rashid and when she saw his dark brows shoot together in a frown she felt a quirk of wry amusement. Obviously the idea of her going to Marrakesh made him furious. And he looked like he could have throttled Jamal for suggesting it.

With a deliberate smile in Rashid's direction she said to Jamal, "Marrakesh? I'd love to go."

"Great! Isn't that great, Rashid? We can fly over on the company plane Thursday afternoon. I'll phone Grandfather tomorrow and tell him we're coming. When do you have to be back, Kathy?"

"Not until Tuesday."

"Four and a half days! Plenty of time for us to show you the city. We might even have time to drive out past the Great Atlas Mountains toward the Sahara." He reached out and took her hand. "There are so many places I want to show you, Kathy."

"And so many things I want to see," she said in a low throaty voice, feeling a ping of satisfaction when her gaze slid from his to Rashid's and she saw a thin white line of anger form around his mouth.

Turning back to Jamal she said, "Thank you for asking, darling. I can hardly wait to leave. I know it's going to be a marvelous four days."

Chapter 4

FOR YEARS THE NAME MARRAKESH HAD STIRRED EXCITE-
ment and longing in Katherine. She had rolled the
name on her tongue, savoring the taste of it. Marrakesh, red city of the Arabian Nights, jewel of the
Islamic world, city of casbahs and *souks*, of snake
charmers and soothsayers, of veiled women with shadowed eyes and henna'd hands.

Sitting in the passenger section of the Learjet with
Jamal, Katherine itched with anticipation. Not even the
tight-lipped expression on Rashid's face ahead of her in
the cockpit could dim her enthusiasm. She wasn't fond
of flying, even in jumbo-sized jets, but there was
something about the way Rashid took command of the
plane that put her at ease. Once they were airborne she
was able to sit back, enjoy the trip and wonder if
Marrakesh would live up to her dream of what the city
was like.

As they flew low, Katherine could see the red houses, the palm trees, the minarets and the mosques. She felt the strange savage beating of her heart and knew that Marrakesh was just as she had imagined it would be.

Although Katherine insisted she would be quite happy at a hotel, Jamal wouldn't hear of it. There was more than enough room at his grandfather's, he said. Besides, the old man would be offended if he and Rashid didn't bring their guest to his home.

Katherine was curious about the man who had taken a French wife and refused to divorce her or take another wife after she left him. He lived in one of the older sections of the city, on the crest of a hill.

The chauffeur, who had picked them up at the airport, drove slowly up the long curved driveway bordered on both sides by stately royal palms. The house, a large two-story pink palace, was surrounded on three sides by terraced gardens, brilliant flowers and fountains that sparkled in the sunlight. As they drew nearer Katherine could see the beautiful tiled Moorish arches.

"Does your grandfather live here alone?" she asked, slightly taken aback by such opulence.

"Just he and the servants," Jamal said. "Of course Rashid and I live here whenever we're in Marrakesh. During the harvest season we're here for two or three months at a time. The family still has olive and orange groves not too far away. Morocco has some of the best oranges in the world. Our family has made its living off them for generations."

The chauffeur opened the door. Jamal helped Katherine alight while Rashid handed the luggage to the two robed men who dashed down the white steps to receive it.

The inside of the house was beautiful and typically Arabian. The floors and walls were tiled in blue and gold mosaic. There was a fountain in the large expanse of foyer, and beyond it Katherine could see Moorish arches leading to other halls and rooms.

Suddenly a man appeared and hurried toward them. Tall and fierce-looking, hair startling white against his bronzed face, he was dressed in a tan-colored djellaba. Rashid went to embrace him, then, holding the older man away, kissed both his cheeks. Then Jamal went to his grandfather and he too kissed him before taking his hand and leading him to Katherine.

"Grandfather, we've brought a guest from the United States, Miss Katherine Bishop. Katherine, this is my grandfather, Youssef Fallah Hasir."

"Miss Bishop." He took her hand as he murmured, *"Marhabán,* welcome. Our house is your house. I hope it pleases you."

"Thank you," Katherine said. "It's kind of you to let me come."

"Have you been to Marrakesh before, Miss Bishop?"

"No, sir, but it's a city I've always wanted to see."

"Then my grandsons will show you around. Rashid, I know Miss Bishop would enjoy the Bahia Palace. It's really lovely, Miss Bishop. The gardens are extraordinary. The scent of jasmine permeates the air this time of year. You really must insist that Rashid take you there tomorrow."

"I imagine Rashid has other plans," Jamal put in, an

odd expression on his face. He placed his arm around Katherine's waist and, smiling down at her, said, "But I'll certainly see that she sees the gardens, Grandfather. Thank you for the suggestion."

The old man's brows drew together in a frown. He glanced from Rashid to Katherine, his dark eyes, so like Rashid's, widening in barely disguised surprise. Then in a smooth voice he said, "Well, my dear, just as long as you see them. And the *souks,* of course. I imagine you'll want to buy a few of the things Marrakesh is famous for. Now I suppose you'd like to freshen up and have your things unpacked. We dine at eight so that will give you an hour or two to rest." He clapped his hands together and when a servant appeared he said, "Show mademoiselle to her room, please."

Youssef Fallah Hasir's home was a far cry from Buckport, Maine, Katherine thought as she followed the servant up a broad marble staircase, then down a long corridor framed with Moorish arches and hung with ornately carved gold lamps. The tiled walls, in intricate star and bursting flower designs, were themselves works of art.

The room the servant led her to was larger than the whole upstairs of the house in Buckport. In the afternoon sun the room was aglow in golden shades of apricot. Gossamer drapes had been pulled back from floor-to-ceiling balcony windows, allowing the sun to brighten the surroundings. The head of the bed, covered by a foamy apricot-colored spread, was draped in gold chiffon. There was a long dresser with a bouquet of yellow roses, a gold velvet chaise, a small desk and chair.

The adjoining bathroom, all white and gold, had a sunken tub, on the side of which were stacks of thick towels, imported soaps and bath oils.

When Katherine came back into the bedroom she went out onto the balcony and looked down at the stretch of terraced gardens below. Beyond the city lay the Atlas Mountains and as she gazed at them Katherine wondered what it was like beyond the mountains, out toward the Sahara. Now that she was away from the capital city of Rabat and the cosmopolitan Casablanca, it seemed to her that she was in the real Morocco. She wanted to explore every inch of Marrakesh. And some day she wanted to see all that lay beyond the Atlas Mountains.

She was glad she'd made this trip with Jamal and Rashid, even though it was obvious Rashid wasn't at all happy about it. The grandfather seemed nice, although he did look like an Arabian chieftan with his dark skin and that shock of white hair. In spite of his age, which she thought to be seventy or so, his body was firm and muscled. His face—so like Rashid's—was strong and manly. She thought she liked him and hoped to get to know him better. But she'd bet every dirham she had that he could be a holy terror when he was angry.

And Youssef Fallah Hasir was angry.

"I thought she belonged to you," he told Rashid after he had sent Jamal out of the room on an errand. "By God, if she doesn't she should. A fine-looking woman. Good lines, splendid legs, wonderful bone structure. And yellow eyes. By God, Rashid, it's been years since I've seen a woman with yellow eyes. Only knew one—a Berber girl from a village near Azrou.

Met her when I was just a teenager and I've never forgotten her." The trace of a smile crossed his lips. "But I don't suppose a man ever forgets the first girl he makes love to.

"It was back in the day when we and the Berbers were always at each other's throats. We'd taken a small village. Most of their men were dead or wounded and after the battle we rounded the women up and put a guard on them. That night some of the men went out to the corral after them. I was the youngest and the men joked and said I'd better stay away because I was only a fuzzy-cheeked boy and I wouldn't know what to do with a woman if I had her."

He rubbed a finger down the length of his nose. "I went out to the corral and I grabbed a girl about my age. A girl with yellow eyes. I can still remember the men laughing when I pulled her out of there, her kicking and hitting and scratching while I tried to drag her away with one hand and protect myself with the other."

Rashid smiled. "She sounds like quite a girl. Were you able to tame her?"

"Tame her? To tell you the truth, boy, I think she tamed me. After I took her I didn't feel anything like I thought I should feel. I was ashamed of myself. I should have let her go back with the other women then, but I couldn't. I don't know how it happened but we made love again, and that time was different. It was good . . . something I'll always remember."

He looked at Rashid and swallowed hard. "That was over fifty years ago. I thought I'd forgotten her until today when I saw your Miss Bishop."

"She's not *my* Miss Bishop."

"If she's not she should be."

"She's Jamal's friend, Grandfather."

"Where'd he meet her?"

"At Princeton. They started dating and when it seemed from his letters that he was serious about her I went over to the States and broke it up. That's when I met her."

"Seven damn years ago?"

Rashid nodded. "By the time I got there she and Jamal were engaged. It was ridiculous, of course, because Jamal was only twenty-one, so I packed him up and sent him home."

"I'm surprised a girl like that let him go without a fight."

"I didn't give her a chance to fight. Jamal was on a plane for Casablanca before she knew anything about it." He didn't add that he'd tried to compensate for Jamal's loss with a check for twenty thousand dollars and that Katherine had flung it in his face. He'd never told anyone because he was ashamed of what he'd done and didn't like to think about it.

"What's she doing here in Morocco?"

"She works for the United States Embassy as an assistant to the vice-consul."

"Jamal trying to take up where he left off?"

"Yes."

"You still don't approve?"

"No, I don't. She's a foreigner, a Christian. A marriage between them would be a mistake—for her as well as for Jamal." Rashid hesitated. "If you'll forgive me, sir, it would be the kind of mistake you made when you married Monique St. Onge."

Youssef's eyes darkened with rage. "Monique Fallah Hasir," he said in a quietly murderous voice. "Your grandmother. My wife. She gave me two fine sons and she loved me. We had eighteen years together and I'll never regret them. There are times, even now, when I think I should go to Paris, grab her by her hair and bring her back here and tie her to the bed until she agrees never to leave me again."

Furious still, Youssef got to his feet and shook a finger in Rashid's face. "At least I haven't been afraid to love," he roared. "What in Allah's name is the matter with you? Can't you see what a fine-looking woman that Bishop girl is? Any fool can see that Jamal isn't man enough for her. But you are. If you had even half a brain in your head you'd know it."

"The woman can't stand me," Rashid said. "Nor I her."

"Camel dung! Make love to her and then see how you feel about each other."

With a grin Rashid said, "Even if I did what you suggest—and let me assure you that I have no intention of doing such a thing—what about Jamal? He's in love with her."

"Damn!" Youssef paced the room. "He's a fine boy, a fine boy. But he's weak, Rashid, and we both know it. He's no match for Miss Bishop. You've got to break them up."

"That's exactly what I'm trying to do. I managed to do it seven years ago, but they're older now. I don't know how successful I'll be."

"I still wish you'd go after her. A woman with yellow eyes is a rare creature."

"Her eyes are golden," Rashid said, almost to himself. Then before his grandfather could say anything else, he excused himself and hurried to his room.

The sound drifted across the early morning air. Strange and haunting, unlike anything Katherine had ever heard. She opened her eyes. It was still dark. She lay for a few minutes, listening to the faintly musical sound, then finally threw back the apricot satin sheet and, slipping into her robe, went out to the balcony.

The city lay below her, surrounded by dull red walls shadowed by the night. Tall palms, like silent sentinels, swayed in the gentle breeze. Minarets pointed to the clouds scudding by. Everything still, everything silent except for the haunting cry that drifted through the stillness.

Suddenly Katherine knew that it was the Moslem call to prayer, that somewhere in the city one lone, ancient and holy man was calling to the faithful through the darkness of the night. She hugged her arms to her body, touched by an excitement she had never known and by the wonder of this place called Marrakesh.

She slept again but woke at seven, too excited by the promise of the city below to go back to sleep. She bathed quickly, then dressed in a cool cotton dress and low-heeled sandals. With her purse over her arm she went silently down the long winding stairs. When a male servant approached she said, *"Bonjour,"* and asked if Jamal had come down.

"No, mademoiselle. No one is about yet. Would you care for breakfast?"

"No, thank you. I'm going out for a while. I'll have breakfast with the others later."

"It's best you don't go out alone, mademoiselle. If

you wait a bit I'm sure one of the gentlemen will accompany you."

"I'll only be an hour or so. I want to see the . . . how do you say it? The Djemaa?"

"The Djemaa El Fna, mademoiselle. But truly, you should not go there alone."

"I'll be perfectly all right. Will you be good enough to call me a taxi?"

"But mademoiselle—"

"Please," she said in a firm voice. "A taxi."

Ten minutes later Katherine arrived at the Djemaa El Fna, the largest *souk* in the world. The mammoth square was crowded. There were monkey trainers, trick cyclists, jugglers and magicians, even a flame eater who called to her as she went by. A variety of musicians, each trying to drown out the others, added to the hodgepodge of noise and confusion. There were whirling dervishes and acrobats, dancers with henna'd hands dressed in folds of cobalt blue and black, their hair bound with silken cloths decorated with jingling silver coins.

Katherine, wide-eyed and breathless, moved slowly through the crowd of entertainers, of men clad in djellabas and veiled women on their way to market. When she heard the sound of a flute she peered around her and saw a gathering of people surrounding a snake charmer. The dark-skinned man, dressed in a white robe and turban, sat cross-legged on the ground. As the high whine of music drifted on the morning air, a cobra, its flat head thrust toward the man, moved its body in rhythm to the music. When at last the snake coiled, the man plunged his hand into a basket at his side and brought out another cobra. The snake spat,

the crowd moved back and Katherine gave an involun-
tary cry of fear. With a shudder, she moved on as the
man began to play his flute.

Suddenly she was confronted by a man dressed in a
strange red suit. He wore a wide felt hat decorated with
red tassels. There were gold cups and bells strung
around his neck, and a goatskin bag draped over his
shoulders.

He said something Katherine didn't understand,
then, taking one of the brass cups, squirted water from
the goatskin into it. When he handed the cup to her she
realized he was the water seller. With a smile she shook
her head, then handed him a dirham.

The minute she did she was surrounded.

"Gold bracelets, lady. Special price for you."

"Wallets? Five dollar. Only five dollar. What'sa
matter? You don't like wallets? I got belts. Ten dollar?"

"Lookit necklace, mademoiselle. Twenty dollar. Fifteen for you. Okay?"

Hands tugged at her arm. Silver necklaces were
thrust in her face.

"You want hashish? I got finest hashish in Marrakesh." A dirty hand shoved a bag at her.

"No! Let me by please."

"Djellaba, lady. Look, like silk. Fit your body like a
glove." A boy about nineteen held a blue robe up
against her, one hand rubbing quickly against her
breast.

Katherine pushed him away, frantic now, and he
cried out, "She hit me. I didn't do nothing and she hit
me."

"I didn't hit you," Katherine protested. "But if you
touch me again I'll knock you senseless!"

She pushed through the crowd, but the sellers pushed after her, attracting others. Katherine was trapped, trapped by the bodies shoving against her, by hands thrust into her face, all trying to sell something, all speaking too fast for her to understand. Suddenly a man in a dirty gray djellaba thrust to the front of the crowd. There was a thin black snake around his neck. He grabbed it with both hands as he came closer, holding it out, high above Katherine's head.

With growing horror she realized he wanted to put it around her neck. She pressed back against the crowd, sick with fear.

"Katherine!"

Over the heads of the men who surrounded her she saw Rashid shoving his way toward her. Crying out, she tried to move toward him as he pushed the men out of the way. He spoke in Arabic, his face angry, hands curled into fists as he knocked aside the man with the snake. Then one strong arm went around her waist and with the other arm he forced a path through the throng of sellers, pulling Katherine with him out of the square into an alley.

"Damn it . . ." he started to say but stopped when Katherine flung herself at him. Her arms went around his neck and she clung to him, shuddering with reaction.

"It's all right," he said roughly. "You're all right now."

When he felt her trembling against him and heard her small gasps of fear he put his hand against her hair. "You're safe now, Katherine," he said. "Nothing is going to hurt you."

She took a deep gulping breath, still clinging to him, and he held her until at last she stepped away.

"I'm sorry," she managed to say. "I was frightened because I couldn't get away from them. Then when I saw that snake . . ."

"I understand. Those street boys can be incredibly aggressive. You have to beat them away with a stick." He put his hands on her shoulders. "Are you sure you're all right? You're as white as a sheet. Ahmed said you didn't have breakfast."

Before Katherine could answer he gave her a small shake. "Damn it, woman, you're not in New York. You should have had better sense than to come out alone. Now come along and let's get you something to eat before you faint."

He took her arm and led her to one side of the square and into a small restaurant alongside the Café de France, then up a flight of stairs onto a roof garden overlooking the Djemaa. He took her to a table, signaled for a waiter and ordered fresh orange juice, hot tea and toast.

"Do you feel better?" he asked after she drank the orange juice.

"Yes, thank you."

"That was a stupid thing you did."

"I know. I'm sorry. It's just that I was so excited about being in Marrakesh. I heard the—is it the call to prayer?—early this morning. I went out on the balcony of my room and it was still dark. The city was so quiet, so mysterious, and I heard this beautiful voice calling out."

"The *Imam*," Rashid said. "The call is made five times each day."

"After that I couldn't wait to see everything. I'd heard about the Djemaa and I had to see it."

"Jamal would have taken you."

"I know." She took a sip of tea. "How did you find me?"

"Ahmed told me where you were going. I raised hell with him for not stopping you."

"He tried to stop me," she protested.

"But you wouldn't listen."

Katherine bit her lip, then with an attempt at a smile said, "Please don't yell at me. I'm not up to it."

A muscle jumped in Rashid's cheek. "All right, I'll wait until you are." With a half-smile he glanced away from her down to the scene below. "It's quite a sight, isn't it?"

Katherine nodded. "I think I like it better from here, though." She looked down at the Djemaa. "How old is it? The city, the square?"

"The city was founded in the eleventh century. It used to be the starting point for the trans-Saharan caravans." He leaned back in his chair and looked down on the square below. "It must have been fascinating hundreds of years ago when the caravans came in from the desert, their goods loaded on camels—gold and silver, jewels, silks, incense and spices, slave girls."

"Slave girls?"

Rashid nodded. "They were sold at auction, right down there in the Djemaa. A man could buy a servant, a cook or—if it was his lucky day—a beauty to add to his harem."

"That's barbaric!"

"Perhaps." Rashid smiled slightly. "Life in the harem wasn't all that bad, Katherine. The women lived in palaces, sheltered from the outside world. They were well fed and they had beautiful clothes, all of the comforts the master could afford."

"What did they have to do in return?" Her voice was sharp with indignation.

"Just please the master." His grin was wicked. "It was a man's world then; a woman had little or no control over her life. In some countries that's still true today."

He took a sip of his tea. "In those days slave traders from Algeria often kidnapped girls from small villages. They were brought here first, then taken to Casablanca and Tangier."

Rashid looked out over the Djemaa, trying to see it as it might have been. There would have been the same snake charmers, the magicians and the storytellers. The same smell of incense and rosewater, the cries of the hawkers, the crush of the crowd. In the center there would have been an auction block. Near it a score of frightened girls, dressed in sheer chiffon and flowing veils, would have waited, trembling in fear for their turn on the block. Their bodies would be perfumed with oils from Persia. The scent of it would linger in the air after they had passed. The men, eyes narrowing, tongues licking heavy lips, would jostle for a place close enough to the block to study each girl as she was brought up, hoping to find a prize he could afford.

What had it been like then? What would it have been like to have found a woman with hair the color of sun-ripened wheat? A woman whose skin was pink-tinged ivory, whose breasts were high and full yet small enough for a man to cup in each of his hands? A woman as tall and slender and graceful as the one sitting across from him now?

He looked into Katherine's eyes, then beyond, beyond into a past that might have been. . . .

He was a merchant on his way back to Tangier, a man with no interest in buying a slave girl. But something had drawn him to the market place. He paused, listening to the auctioneer. He had already turned away when they brought her out. She was taller than the others and through the drape of lavender chiffon he saw the sweet lushness of her body and felt as though he had received a blow to his heart.

He stood frozen, gazing up at her. Then he saw the grossly fat man dressed in a soiled robe, a ring on each of his sausage fingers, step forward to bid. Almost without knowing that he did, he topped the fat man's bid.

Up and up went the price and the fat man's small pig eyes narrowed in anger. He gazed at the girl, licking his thick red lips, then glared at his opponent and cried, "Ten thousand dirham."

"Twenty thousand," he said. And she was his.

The crowd hushed. Up on the block the girl with the golden eyes turned and looked down at him. Her eyes were narrowed in hate, her fists clenched in anger, and he knew she would be as difficult to tame as the Berber girl his grandfather had taken. It would take all of his strength to mold her into the woman he wanted her to be. He would have to be forceful, perhaps even cruel, but eventually she would be his.

He'd dress her in the finest silks from the Orient, adorn her in jewels. She would have his sons, she . . .

"Rashid?"

He looked at Katherine with eyes blinded by his fantasy. What was the matter with him? He rubbed a hand across his face. What kind of a spell had she cast over him to make him dream such a dream?

Abruptly he pushed his chair back. "If you're feeling better we'll go. Jamal is probably crazy with worry." He put his hand out for hers, then quickly drew back. "We can get a taxi downstairs. You're all right now, aren't you?"

"Yes, thank you. And thank you for rescuing me, Rashid. I don't know what I'd have done if you hadn't found me."

"Just don't try anything that stupid again." His voice was sharper than he had meant it to be and for a moment, when he saw her white teeth clamp down on her lower lip and the flush of color creep into her cheeks, he wanted to say, I didn't mean it, Katherine.

He wanted to take her hand in his and tell her that he was sorry, that he didn't mean to be so harsh—but that when she looked at him with her great golden eyes he couldn't think. He couldn't even breathe properly. All he could do was snap at her and then take her safely back to his brother.

Chapter 5

JAMAL, HIS FACE TAUT WITH WORRY, PUT HIS ARMS around Katherine and said, "Thanks be to Allah that you're all right."

But Youssef Fallah Hasir shouted at her and told her she had done a damn fool thing. Then he insisted she have a sip of his very best French brandy, which he kept only for medicinal purposes since everyone knew that Moslems didn't drink, and made her sit down to a breakfast of steak and eggs.

"You foolish girl," he admonished, watching each bite she put into her mouth. "You might have been hurt. The sellers in the *souks* are the most ferocious in the world. Here, drink your tea while it's hot." He held the cup to her lips.

"Women in Morocco don't go alone to such places. I myself would have taken you if you had asked. Tell me and I'll see to it that you go anywhere you wish, see anything you want to see, but I simply will not allow you to wander about alone. Here, let me peel you an orange."

Katherine was torn between telling him that she was quite capable of taking care of herself in *most* situations, and grabbing him by his ears and kissing both his cheeks. Instead she listened with more patience than she usually was capable of to all his admonishments and meekly accepted the sections of orange when he handed them to her.

That afternoon, after she had rested, Jamal took her back to the Djemaa. He ran interference, bargaining with the sellers in Arabic, helping her with her purchases. She bought a djellaba, a caftan and several pairs of jeweled slippers. Finally, arms loaded with packages, she and Jamal returned to the house.

"Shall I wear my new caftan tonight?" she asked him.

"Yes, Grandfather would like that. He's rather lonely for female company and I know he enjoys having you here."

"He's a tough old lion, isn't he?" she said with a smile. "It's a shame about your grandmother. How long has she lived in Paris?"

"For almost twenty years."

"They haven't seen each other in all that time?"

"They've seen each other occasionally, whenever Granddad's been in Paris. The last time was a few years ago. It's too bad they've been separated, Kathy, because I know he still loves her. But they're both so stubborn. He thinks she was wrong and that it's up to her to come to him, and she refuses to budge out of Paris. He's from the old school and doesn't accept the fact that things are changing here in Morocco. He still expects Grandmother to be robed and veiled. She refused twenty years ago and she still refuses."

"But a lot of women aren't veiled."

"I know, but my grandfather won't accept the new ways. He thinks a woman should be secluded in the home, that she shouldn't venture out unless her husband accompanies her and that the only time her face and figure should be seen is when they're alone or with family. Actually, my grandfather isn't the only one who feels that way. A lot of men still do. Rashid is one of them."

"Somehow that doesn't surprise me."

"That's probably why he never married. Most Moroccan women today are far too modern to ever accept such an arrangement."

"And of course he'd never marry a foreigner."

"Never!"

"What about you, Jamal? How do you feel about women being veiled? Do you plan to keep your wife covered from head to toe with layers of cloth?"

Jamal flushed and for a moment looked away from her. Then with his slow sweet smile he said, "I'd never ask you to wear a veil. If you were my wife you'd be free to do almost anything you wanted to do." He put his arms around her. "I still want to marry you, Kathy," he said softly.

"Jamal, please. It's too soon to talk about marriage. We've been apart for a long time. We've both changed."

"I haven't changed, darling. At least not in the way I feel about you."

"Let's not talk about it now, Jamal, all right?" She

slipped out of his arms. "What did you do when you left Princeton? Did you finish your education here in Morocco?"

"No, I went to the Sorbonne. I was so damned mad at Rashid that I refused to go to the university here. That's when Rashid decided I should try the Sorbonne."

"Rashid!" Katherine couldn't stop the sharp reply that tumbled from her lips. "My God, Jamal, you were twenty-one. Couldn't you have picked your own school?"

"Rashid controlled my part of the family money until I was twenty-five, Kathy. There wasn't anything I could do."

She thought of the $20,000 check she had flung in Rashid's face.

Trying to hide her sudden feeling of disdain she turned away, but when she started out of the room Jamal said, "Please, Kathy, it happened seven years ago. I'm sorry I wasn't man enough to stand up to Rashid then. Believe me when I tell you how much I've regretted what I did. All I can tell you now is that I'll never let him or anybody else come between us again."

Katherine looked at him. She felt confused, not really sure what her feelings were. But when she started to speak he said, "Don't say anything now, darling." Drawing her into his arms he kissed her, murmuring against her lips, "My sweet Kathy," and she could feel his body warm with desire.

She pulled away from him, but then, because he looked like an injured child, she turned back and rested her hands on his shoulders. "Don't look so sad, Jamal," she said.

"I can't help it, Kathy. I want you, I want you so much I can barely stand it."

Suddenly, behind him, she saw Rashid standing in the doorway. His eyes were cold, his mouth drawn into a thin line of disapproval.

Katherine's hands tightened on Jamal's shoulders. Turning her gaze from Rashid she kissed Jamal lightly on his lips and said, "We'll talk later, darling," in a voice loud enough for Rashid to hear.

For dinner that night Katherine wore her new caftan of ivory and gold brocade. Her wheat-colored hair was pulled back from her face by a thin gold band and hung straight and smooth down her back. Her only jewelry was a pair of gold loop earrings.

"I've made a shaker of martinis," Youssef said when he greeted her. Taking her hand he led her into a beautifully appointed salon. "I happen to know that Rashid, for all his sterling qualities, has a weakness for gin and vermouth. I've made enough for the two of you. Jamal and I are made of sterner stuff, so we'll settle for Perrier."

Katherine smiled as she took the drink he offered. When she took a sip she said, "This is marvelous, Mr. Hasir. I think it's the best martini I've ever had."

"Holland gin, Miss Bishop. I'll give you a case when you leave."

"No, no please. I can't accept such a gift."

"Of course you can and you will. Now come over here and sit beside me. I want to know where you come from in the United States and what you think of Morocco."

It was a pleasant evening. Youssef was a wonderful

host and the food was some of the best Katherine had ever eaten. After dinner, because the evening air was pleasantly warm, they went out to the patio where coffee was served.

"Smell the jasmine," Youssef said. "It's particularly aromatic this time of year." Taking Katherine's arm he said, "Let me show you the view from over here," and led her away from the others to where they could see the lights of the city.

"I love Marrakesh," he murmured. "But as I get older I find that I like it best from a distance. There are too many people down there for me. I know it must have been frightening for you this morning."

"Yes, it was."

"I'm glad Rashid found you." He hesitated. "Do you like it here in Morocco, Miss Bishop?"

"Yes, I do. I think it's a fascinating country. I'm glad I came."

"How long will you be here? I know you're working for the embassy in Rabat, but I don't know how long these assignments are."

"They could be anywhere from two years to five or six years."

"Will you be content to stay that long?"

"Yes, I'm sure I will."

"You don't miss your parents?"

"I miss them very much, but we write often. I'll see them for a month next year when I go home for leave."

"What do they think about your being so far away? Especially your father, what does he think?"

"My father knows I'm a capable, mature woman, sir, and that I have to find my own way in the world."

"Americans! And for Allah's sake stop calling me

sir. My name is Youssef." His keen dark eyes searched her face. Then abruptly he asked, "Are you going to marry Jamal?"

For a moment Katherine was too startled to speak. Then she said, "I don't know. I'm . . . I'm not sure."

"You were going to marry him seven years ago."

"Yes."

"And now?"

"Maybe."

"That's what I was afraid of."

"Because I'm an American?"

"No, damn it, because you'll be marrying the wrong grandson."

Katherine stared at him, her eyes wide with shock. "What . . . what do you mean?"

"You know damn well what I mean. Rashid's the man for you, not Jamal. Hell, you'll walk all over Jamal and make him like it. But you couldn't do that with Rashid. If you married him you'd have a man who could handle you."

Katherine's eyes narrowed dangerously. "Handle me? *Bully* me, you mean. I'd never let a man do that. I'd fight him every inch of the way."

"Would you now?"

"You're absolutely right I would."

His smile was sly. "I knew you'd say that. I knew those yellow tiger eyes of yours would narrow and spit fire. Lord girl, but you remind me . . ." He shook his head, took a deep steadying breath and said, "You've got spirit, Miss Katherine, and I admire that in a woman. I know you think I'm an interfering old man, but I can't help myself. I love both of my grandsons and I want what's best for them. I just happen to think you'd be the best thing that ever happened to Rashid and that he'd be good for you. But I suppose it's none of my business. Now let's get back to the others."

But when Katherine moved to go he took hold of her arm, stopping her for a moment. "You think about what I said," he told her in a low voice. "But remember that whatever happens I'd be proud to have you for my granddaughter, even if you are an American."

"Thank you, I think," she said with a slow smile. Then she slipped her arm through his and went back to where Jamal and Rashid waited.

Katherine saw Jamal often in the days following her return from Marrakesh. Although his office was in Tangier, he came to both Casablanca and Rabat for business at least once or twice a week and every weekend. He was attentive and loving, but every time he began to work his way around to the subject of marriage she managed to sidestep it and talk about something else.

She knew she wouldn't be able to do that much longer. She wasn't sure what held her back. Jamal hadn't changed from the young man she'd loved when she was twenty. He was still a gentle man, tender and loving, obviously in love with her. Although he made it quite clear that he desperately wanted to make love to her, he hadn't pressed when Katherine resisted. He loved her and he wanted to marry her, and she really wasn't sure why she held back. But at last, as she had known it would, the time came when the subject could no longer be avoided.

They had spent the evening dining and dancing and

when they returned to her apartment Jamal asked if he could come in.

"Only for a minute," Katherine said. "I have a heavy day tomorrow."

"What I have to say will only take a minute," he said as he followed her in. Before she could snap a light on he pulled her into his arms. "I love you," he whispered against her hair. "I love the scent of you, the feel of you." With a soft groan of need his mouth found hers as his arms tightened around her. "I can't endure this," he murmured against her lips. "Being with you, touching you and still not having you."

"Jamal—"

"Don't keep punishing me for what I did seven years ago, Kathy. I'm not asking you to have an affair with me. I want you to be my wife. Oh Kathy, I love you so."

She wanted to weep because he was so dear and because she had loved him once. "I don't know what to say." Her voice was gentle. "I'm not sure I'm ready for marriage, Jamal."

"Is there anyone else?"

"No, of course not."

"Then I have a chance. That's all I ask, Kathy. Just a chance." He kissed her eyelids, her nose, the corners of her mouth. "My sweet darling," he murmured. "Tell me you love me, Kathy. Please tell me you love me."

"Jamal . . ." Perhaps it was because of what had once been between them. Perhaps it was because of his trembling need that she closed her eyes and whispered, "I love you, Jamal."

"Oh, darling." He kissed her again. "You'll marry

me?" Before Katherine could answer he covered her mouth with his, stopping her protests with a kiss.

When he released her he said, "Let's make it soon; I'll go crazy if I have to wait much longer. Next week? Next month? Where would you like to be married? How about Marrakesh? Grandfather would love it if we got married there. Let's call him right now."

Katherine stepped out of his arms. Her head spun; she wasn't even sure what had happened. "Why don't we . . ." Her voice died. "Why don't we wait a while before we . . . before we tell anybody."

Jamal laughed and reached for her again. "But I want to tell everybody. I want to tell the whole world." He caught her around the waist and swept her off her feet. "I want everybody to know you're mine. Oh God, Kathy, I'm so happy."

She tried to smile, tried to tell herself that she was as happy as he was. But after he left she sat in the dark for a long time, hands clenched in her lap, wondering what she was going to do.

Chapter 6

"I HAVE A PRESENT FOR YOU, KATHY," JAMAL SAID TWO nights later as he handed her a gift-wrapped package. Then he smiled across the table at Rashid. "It's something special, big brother. I wanted you to be here when I gave it to her."

"What's the occasion?" Nervously Katherine fingered the red ribbon.

"Just open it, darling. You'll see."

Aware of Rashid watching her every movement, Katherine slipped the satin ribbon off the package. "I can't imagine what it is," she murmured, wishing Jamal hadn't done this in front of his brother. She opened the box and, pushing away the layers of white tissue, saw a beautiful wide gold belt, so obviously expensive it took her breath. As she lifted it out of the folds of tissue she heard Rashid gasp.

"It's lovely!" she said.

"But you don't know what it is, do you?" Jamal asked.

"It's a belt." Katherine looked at him, a puzzled expression on her face.

"A very special belt, Kathy." Jamal covered her hand with his. "It's a marriage belt."

"A marriage belt?" She still didn't understand.

"It's our custom," Rashid said in a cold voice. "When a couple becomes engaged the man gives the woman a gold marriage belt, the most expensive he can afford. I'd say this one is very expensive."

"Very!" Jamal laughed.

"It's a form of security," Rashid explained in the same cold voice, "like having money in the bank. Later in the marriage, if they need to, the couple can always sell it."

"We'll never sell this one." Jamal squeezed her hand.

She looked from brother to brother, not knowing what to say or what to do. She felt trapped. It was official now. Jamal had announced their engagement and she wasn't even sure she'd said yes.

"When's the wedding?" Rashid asked.

"Next month—if that's all right with Katherine. If I had my way we'd be married tomorrow, but I suppose there are things to be arranged. How do you think Grandfather will feel about having the wedding in Marrakesh? I think he'd be pleased, don't you?"

"Probably." Rashid looked across the table at Katherine. "What about you? Is that where you'd like to be married?"

"I . . ." She swallowed nervously. "Yes, of course, if that's what Jamal wants."

"So you're already beginning to practice our ways." There was only the slightest hint of irony in Rashid's voice. "The dutiful fiancée, acceding to her beloved's wishes. I find that quite touching."

Katherine lifted her chin. "Most women want to please the men they love," she said, and saw his eyes darken with anger.

"You do love Jamal, of course."

Her gaze, still caught by his, faltered as her hands tightened around the marriage belt. "Of course I love him," she managed to say. "Why else would I agree to marry him?"

"Why indeed, Miss Bishop?"

"All right, you two, that's enough," Jamal broke in. He smiled at Katherine. "You do like your present, don't you, darling?"

"Yes, Jamal. I'll treasure it always."

"You'll wear it at our wedding?"

Her pause was almost imperceptible. Then she took a deep breath and with a nod said, "Of course, Jamal. Of course I'll wear it at our wedding."

The following evening, as Katherine dressed to go out with him, Jamal phoned.

"Bad luck, Kathy," he said. "I've got to fly to Tangier tonight."

"Tonight? I'm sorry, Jamal. When will you be back?"

"I'm not sure. I may have to go on to Paris."

"Paris!"

"Company business, sweetheart. I can't get out of it. Rashid would go but he's tied up with a government meeting next week."

"I see."

"There's really nobody except me who can take care of it."

"How long will you be gone?"

"That's the rotten part. Rashid says I may have to go on to Lyon from Paris."

Rashid. Her hand tightened on the phone.

"I'll be away at least a week, maybe two. I'm sorry, Kathy, there just isn't anything I can do about it."

"I understand." Oh yes, she thought. I understand.

"Have you written your parents yet?"

"No, but I will."

"Maybe they can come for the wedding."

"I doubt it."

"If it's a question of money we can send them the tickets."

"We'll talk about it when you return."

"All right, Kathy. Look, I've got to go. Rashid's going to drive me to the airport. I'll call in a few days."

"All right, darling. Have a safe trip."

When she put the phone down she stood for a moment, her face twisted in anger. Rashid had done it again! And quite successfully too. He'd keep Jamal away as long as he could, long enough at least to give him a chance to see how he could ruin their marriage plans. Damn him!

Jamal phoned her from Paris, then from Lyon to say he had to fly to Geneva. "It can't be helped, Kathy. We do a tremendous export business in olives this time of year. There's trouble with shipments and apparently I'm the only one who can straighten it out."

"Apparently."

"It looks like we'll have to postpone the wedding, at least for a few weeks. Will it make any difference in your job?"

"I don't think so."

"You have told them you're leaving, haven't you?"

"No."

Her job was the only thing they argued about. Katherine wanted to stay on at the embassy after they married, but Jamal wanted her to quit. "I want you to be a full-time wife," he said.

"I'll be a full-time wife," she had replied. "But I've worked for this assignment. I love what I do and I think it's important." Now, hearing the edge of anger in his voice, she said, "We'll talk about it when you come back."

"All right, but please remember how I feel about your working after we're married."

"I'll remember."

"I've got to run, darling. I'm sure I'll be back by the middle of next week."

But he wasn't. He phoned from Geneva to say that Rashid had just called to tell him to get back to Lyon. He was leaving the hotel and rushing to the airport. He'd call her from Lyon.

When she put the phone down she was angry, angry at Jamal for being too blind to see what Rashid was up to, and at Rashid for doing the same thing he'd done seven years ago. But mixed with her anger was a feeling of relief. The wedding would have to be delayed. They couldn't make any plans until Jamal returned.

Katherine had never felt so uncertain, so confused. Everything had happened too fast. She should never have accepted the marriage belt that sealed the engagement. And she wouldn't have if Rashid hadn't been sitting across the table from her. She'd looked at the belt, then at him, and all of the long-ago hurt had come rushing back. It had seemed to her that they were not in Rabat but instead back at Princeton at another restaurant and he was handing her a check for $20,000 and saying, "And to help ease the pain of losing Jamal."

His voice had taunted her, daring her to refuse the money. Just as his eyes had taunted her about the marriage belt. Heaven help her, she'd accepted the belt to prove he could no longer tell her or Jamal how to run their lives.

She knew, of course, that Rashid had deliberately sent Jamal away and that he would keep him away for as long as he could in the hope that somehow he would be able to break them up. So she was surprised at the end of that week when Rashid called to tell her Jamal had made plans to return to Morocco. "He'll be flying directly to Marrakesh," Rashid said. "He wants you to meet him there."

"In Marrakesh?" Katherine frowned into the phone. "Why didn't he call me himself?"

"He didn't have time. Said he was running for the plane when he called. Look, I told him I was flying to Marrakesh in the morning and he asked me to call to see if you'd fly with me. Can you take a few days off? The weekend's coming up. Jamal has earned a vacation. It would do you both good to take it easy for a few days."

Katherine stared at the telephone in disbelief. Was Rashid actually trying to be nice to her?

"I'm not sure," she said slowly. "But yes, I suppose I

could take a couple of days off. What time did you plan to leave in the morning?"

"About nine, if that's not too early for you."

"No, nine will be all right."

"Take lightweight clothes. Marrakesh can be hot this time of year. I'll come by for you at eight."

"Thank you. It will be nice to see your grandfather again."

"And Jamal?" His voice mocked her. "Won't it be nice to see Jamal?"

"Of course! I only meant . . ." She took a deep breath and in a cool voice said, "I'll see you in the morning, Rashid," replacing the phone a bit harder than was necessary.

Rashid was polite. He asked Katherine if she would like to sit next to him in the cockpit. She said no, that she preferred not to see things that clearly.

"Afraid of flying?"

"A bit."

"It's quite safe." He led her to a window seat. "Can I get you a drink or anything?"

"No thank you." The thought of a drink or anything else before a flight made her queasy. All she'd had this morning was a cup of tea.

She sat back, trying to dispel a feeling of foreboding as she fastened her seat belt. She didn't like being alone with Rashid but she consoled herself by remembering that Jamal would be in Marrakesh when she arrived and that when she saw him all of the misgivings she'd felt while he was gone would vanish. She'd ask him to delay the wedding for another month and perhaps she would invite her parents to come to Morocco after all.

The steady drone of the plane soothed her as she leafed through a magazine. Finally she put it aside, closed her eyes and drifted off to sleep. When she woke she glanced at her watch, surprised to see it was almost noon. They should be arriving in Marrakesh any minute. She glanced out the window and saw the close rise of mountains. She hadn't remembered crossing the mountains on the other trip to Marrakesh, but perhaps she'd been too excited to notice.

Fifteen minutes went by. With growing impatience Katherine drummed her fingernails against the magazine she'd tried to read. They should have been approaching Marrakesh by now and all she could see was mountains and desert. She had just started up out of her seat to ask Rashid how much longer it would be before they reached their destination when the "Fasten Seat Belt" sign flashed on. Katherine settled back into her seat, sighing with relief. He'd approached from another direction, something about wind currents probably. Marrakesh must be right below them.

But when she looked out of the plane there was no sign of the city.

The plane flew lower, then lower still. My God, Katherine thought, what's happening? Is something wrong with the plane? Were they going to crash? Why hadn't Rashid warned her? Why hadn't he said something?

She saw the runway then, a narrow strip only wide enough to handle a plane as small as this one. The wheels touched down and the plane glided along the runway, slowed and finally came to a stop.

Ahead of her she saw a hangar. To the side of the runway she saw a car.

Rashid turned the engine off and swiveled to face her. "We're here," he said in a flat voice.

"Here? Where?" Katherine's voice climbed two octaves. She bit her lip, trying to quell her fright. "Where is here?"

"The other side of the Atlas Mountains, Katherine."

"But why did you land? Is something wrong with the plane? Jamal is waiting in Marrakesh."

Rashid shook his head. "Jamal is in Lyon. He'll be there until I tell him to come home."

"What are you talking about?" She wanted to shake him. "Why did you tell me we were flying to Marrakesh?" Her eyes were wide as a sudden and terrible fear gripped her. Oh God! She should have known better than to have come with Rashid. He hated her. He'd do anything to keep her from marrying Jamal. Anything.

"What are you going to do to me?" she whispered.

"Do to you?" He towered over her, his cruelly sensuous mouth curved into a smile. "I'm not going to *do* anything to you. You're going to be my guest for a while, that's all."

"Your guest?" She stared up at him in disbelief. "You can't do this," she said at last.

"Can't I? In a few days Wade Contney will receive a telegram, sent from Marrakesh of course, telling him that you and Jamal have gone to Agadir for a week or two. Jamal will receive a telegram too, telling him you've been sent to another embassy for a while and that you'll be in touch."

He reached out and pulled her to her feet. "Nobody's going to worry about you, Katherine, because nobody knows you're with me."

"You can't do this. This is . . . kidnapping! It's—"

"Kidnapping? Don't be silly—you're practically a member of the family. I've brought you here so we can talk, that's all. I'm not going to harm you."

"You've brought me here to talk!" Her voice rose hysterically. "My God, Rashid, you could have talked to me in Rabat."

"But you wouldn't have listened to me there. Here you'll have to." He picked up her suitcase, then gripping her arm said, "Now, will you come along quietly or shall I drag you out?"

Her yellow eyes narrowed to slits. "Can you even imagine how much I hate you?" she said in a low voice.

For a moment it seemed that he flinched. Then his grip on her arm tightened and he shoved her ahead of him to the door of the plane.

Chapter 7

THE HEAT HIT KATHERINE LIKE A PHYSICAL BLOW AND THE sun blinded her. When she shaded her eyes with her hand she saw two men get out of a black Mercedes sedan. Dressed in djellabas, they looked strong and capable. Their faces were lined and bronzed by the sun, their bodies gnarled and tough.

"Marhabán," one of the men said, "Welcome. It is cool in the car. Fakhout and I will attend to the plane."

"Shûkrún, Saoud, thank you. Is everything prepared at the house?"

"Everything awaits you as always, *sidi."*

Rashid nodded. He took Katherine's arm and led her to the car. "Get in the back," he ordered.

"You'll never get away with this, Rashid. I'm an employee of the United States Embassy. There's going to be hell to pay when they discover I'm missing."

"I've handled that."

"What about Jamal? Have you handled that too? What do you think he'll do when he discovers what you've done? It will be the end of your relationship. He'll never forgive you."

His hand tightened on her arm. "Get in," he said again.

"Where are we?" she demanded when she was in the car. "Where are you taking me?"

"I have a home near the edge of the Sahara. That's where we're going. You'll find it's quite comfortable. There are all the amenities, but if there's anything special you desire you have only to ask."

"I'm asking now. I'm asking you to fly me out of here and back to Rabat."

"After we've had a chance to talk."

"Rashid, please . . ." She took a deep shaking breath, trying not to let him know how frightened she was. "I know you don't like me, that you haven't liked me since the first time you saw me seven years ago. I'm not sure why. Maybe it's because I'm an American and a Christian. Maybe you think I'll try to change Jamal. But I won't. I'm quite willing to live in his country, to—"

"To live like a Moroccan woman?" Rashid cut in. "To accept all the Moroccan customs?"

"No, of course not. But Jamal wouldn't ask me to do that."

"Are you so sure, Katherine?" He turned away, cutting the conversation, and they sat in silence until the two men secured the plane and came back to the car.

They were at the edge of the Sahara, Rashid had

said, south of the Atlas Mountains, in the land of the Berbers. But why? Dear God, why had he brought her here?

With the man Saoud at the wheel they drove past small villages where red houses stood baking in the sun. The land was flat and dry. A few scrub plants grew among the stones and rocks. Sand dunes lay on either side of the narrow road.

Katherine tried to memorize the few signs she saw. Rashid might think he was going to keep her here against her will, but sooner or later she'd find a way to get away from him. When she did she had to know where to go.

"Are we near a town?" she asked, keeping her voice casual.

He nodded. "Erfoud. It's the gateway to the Sahara, larger than most of the other towns in this region."

Erfoud. She tucked the name away in her memory.

In a little while they turned off the main road onto an even narrower private road. Now, on either side, there was nothing but miles and miles of sand for as far as she could see.

Katherine glanced at her watch. When Rashid said, "There, to the left, that's the house," she looked at it again. They'd been on this private road almost thirty-five minutes.

For a moment all she could see was sand, but at last she saw the oasis and finally, rimmed with tall palms, the house that was almost the same pink-red color as the sand.

Hands clenched, unable to believe this was happening, Katherine watched the approach to the house with growing fear. Never in her life had she been in a situation where she felt so helpless. There was no one to whom she could appeal for help. The men in the front seat worked for Rashid. Even if she spoke their language they wouldn't have listened to her pleas. If she managed to get away from Rashid where could she run? She gazed around her in growing panic. The oasis was isolated in a sea of sand. There was nothing for miles around.

Stay calm, she told herself. Look around, try to find something that might help you.

There was what looked like a small river running through the oasis. Off to one side was a grove of orange trees. There were also date palms and fig trees. On the other side there appeared to be a village of perhaps a dozen or so adobe houses. Women stood in small clusters near the buildings. They were robed and veiled; children played near them in the dirt.

When the car stopped the children ran to circle it, jumping up and down in excitement, their faces wreathed in smiles as they shouted, *"Marhabán, sidi, marhabán."* They stared in the window at Katherine, poking each other and laughing as they gazed at her.

Rashid got out and offered her his hand. Ignoring it, Katherine got out by herself. She glanced around her. To her right was an open two-car garage. Inside there was a jeep. Back beyond that, under a stand of palm trees, she saw a corral and near it what looked like a stable.

"Come along," Rashid said. He handed her suitcase to one of the woman servants.

"Fatima will show you to your room," he told Katherine. "She's Berber, as are all these people. She doesn't speak French or English and almost no Arabic, so it won't do you any good to try to communicate with her. When you're ready she'll escort you to the dining room."

"In chains?" With one angry glance Katherine turned to follow the woman Fatima into the house.

The foyer, with its Moorish arches and sparkling-clean tile floor, led up a small flight of stairs to what was obviously the living room. There were several luxuri-ously large sofas, low carved tables covered with bright mosaic tiles, straight-back chairs, hassocks and book-cases. Circular fans whirred overhead.

Whatever Rashid used this hideaway house of his for he had obviously spared no expense, Katherine thought as she followed Fatima down a long corridor. Finally the Berber woman stopped in front of an eight-foot-high carved door, then, bowing to Katherine, she opened it to reveal one of the most beautiful bedrooms Katherine had ever seen.

It was a golden room; everything in it was gold and ivory. The only touch of color was a turquoise velvet chaise and turquoise decorator pillows on the ivory brocade spread covering the round bed. Everything else in the room—the thick-pile carpet, the gossamer drapes, the furniture, the desert paintings hanging on the walls—was done in tones of ivory and gold.

If this was a prison, Katherine thought with wonder, then surely it was the most beautiful prison in the world.

She ran her hand across the dresser, touched the petals of the white roses in the vase at one end, then moved to the dressing table. On it was a matching silver mirror, comb and brush set monogrammed with the initial *K*. She stared at it, the breath catching in her throat. *K* for Katherine? Had this room, this *prison*, been designed for her?

With trembling fingers she touched unopened bottles of French perfume and a completely outfitted makeup case. Impossible! Yet it was as though everything in this room had been arranged for her.

Terror took hold of her then. Cold unreasoning terror that she tried with every ounce of her willpower to control.

The woman Fatima spoke to her and for the first time Katherine really looked at the Berber woman. Fatima was dressed in a dark homespun robe. Her hair was covered but she wasn't veiled. She had nice eyes and a warm smile; if it hadn't been for the tattooed stars on both cheeks she could have been from anywhere in the world.

This isn't real, Katherine thought. Any moment now I'm going to wake up in my own room back in Buckport. Then Fatima said something Katherine didn't understand, and crossing the room she opened a door and motioned Katherine inside to a bathroom that was all turquoise and gold tile.

A built-in bench curved all around one side. There was a double sink with indirect lighting, a built-in hairdryer, shelves stacked with thick towels and at one end of the room, in front of floor-to-ceiling windows that Katherine hoped were two-way glass, was a sunken turquoise bathtub. On a wicker stand beside the tub were several kinds of unopened bath oils and French soaps.

Fatima reached down and turned the golden fish-shaped faucets. Then she opened one of the bottles of bath oil and splashed it into the water.

"All right," Katherine said in a shaky voice. "Maybe a bath will make me feel better."

Fatima smiled, then went out and closed the door. Katherine stripped out of her clothes. She sat on the edge of the tub, dangling her feet in the scented foam before she finally lowered herself into the water.

When Fatima knocked fifteen minutes later she came in with a white satin robe. Motioning Katherine out of the tub, she handed her a towel. After Katherine had dried herself and slipped into the robe, she followed Fatima back into the bedroom. When she didn't see her suitcase she said, "Where are my clothes?"

Fatima looked puzzled, then a light dawned and she crossed the room and opened sliding doors to reveal a closet filled with djellabas and caftans.

"No!" Hands on her hips, Katherine glared at the woman. *"My* clothes. I want *my* clothes."

But Fatima only smiled. Taking Katherine's hand, she led her to the dresser and opened the drawers. Inside, carefully folded, was an array of the sheerest and surely the most expensive underwear Katherine had ever seen—lace bras, satin bikini panties, garter belts, teddies, slips. And nightgowns that looked as though they had been spun from fairy cloth.

Katherine stared at Fatima. The woman nodded, pointed to the clothes and then to Katherine.

What in the hell was going on? Katherine pushed her long hair back from her face. She felt dizzy with fright. And hot, so hot. How did people live in this climate? How did they breathe? She couldn't think. She couldn't understand. . . . This room had so obviously been designed to please a woman. Was she the woman?

In spite of the heat a shiver ran through her body.

She swayed and felt Fatima's hand on her arm. Through a misty haze she saw the concern on the woman's face.

Fatima pointed to Katherine's watch, then to her stomach. Then she led her to the dresser and pointed to the underwear. *"Yallah, yallah,"* she said.

Katherine took a deep steadying breath and the dizziness passed. Angrily she snatched a pair of pale blue panties and a matching bra from the drawer, then went to the closet and chose a blue silk caftan. When she pointed to her feet Fatima slid back the doors of a smaller wardrobe and Katherine saw racks and racks of jeweled Moroccan slippers.

"Oh for heaven's sweet sake!" she said when Fatima handed her a pair. She snatched them from the Berber woman and went behind the screen to dress. The bra fit her perfectly, as did the panties and the caftan. Again Katherine felt a chill of fear.

After she'd brushed her hair and applied a touch of makeup she turned to Fatima and said, "I'm as ready as I'll ever be," and followed the woman out of the room and down the long corridor to the dining room where Rashid waited.

He had changed from the dark business suit he had been wearing to a white djellaba.

"I've had a small table set up in the alcove where it's cooler," he said when he saw her. "It takes a while to adjust to the heat."

Katherine didn't answer.

"Would you care for something to drink? Fresh orange juice perhaps?"

She nodded.

He said something to one of the servants who

hovered nearby, and to Katherine said, "Come, sit down."

She did as he asked because she knew she had no choice. Accepting the drink from the servant she took a tentative sip and said, "Rashid, please, let's stop this nonsense and talk."

"After we have finished our drinks."

Katherine stared at him helplessly. She wanted to throttle him. To throw herself at him and pummel him with her fists and wipe that calm, totally composed expression off his face. But all she could do was turn away and stare out at the garden while she sipped her orange juice.

When she finished, the servants served a lunch of a fresh green salad and broiled chicken. It looked appetizing but Katherine couldn't eat. It was too oppressively hot and she was too upset. She picked at her food and Rashid finally said, "You don't like the chicken? Would you prefer something else?"

"No! What I'd prefer is for you to stop acting so damn civilized." She felt the dampness of her face and dabbed at it with her napkin. "If you're a barbarian then act like one, damn it. That would be easier to understand than this . . . this opulence."

He looked quietly amused. "So you think I'm a barbarian?"

"Aren't you? You've kidnapped me, brought me here to this . . . this desert hideaway of yours. I don't know what you plan to do with me."

He sighed and pushed his plate back. "I see we're not to eat in peace." He clapped his hands and a servant took away the plates. Then he turned to Katherine and said, "Very well, we'll talk if that's what you want."

"You said you brought me here to talk about Jamal and me," she said. "About our upcoming marriage. You could have done that back in Rabat, but you've gone to rather elaborate pains to bring me here. You've sent Jamal to France, and you've told my embassy I've taken a vacation I didn't request and which will probably cost me my job." Her eyes were intent on his. "This wasn't a spur-of-the-moment decision, Rashid. You've planned this very carefully."

"Very carefully."

"The clothes." Katherine fingered the silk material of the caftan. "This, the other things, the shoes. Who do they belong to? Do you keep them for the women you bring here? Do you have a mistress?"

He shook his head. "Not yet."

A frantic frightened pulse beat in her throat. She tried to look away but could not. She was snared by the intense blackness of his eyes.

"You know that everything is for you, Katherine," he said in a soft voice.

"But why? Why?"

"I think you know that too, Katherine. Katherine Bishop of Buckport, Maine, whose father has a drugstore on the corner of Fifth and Market streets, whose mother taught kindergarten at the Abraham Lincoln Elementary School before she married. That's where you went to school. There and Buckport High School where you were the valedictorian of your class and graduated with honors high enough to get a partial scholarship to Princeton."

"How did you . . . ?" Her eyes were wide with shock.

"How did I find out these things? It's easy when one has enough money and enough interest to dig a bit."

He leaned back, watching her as he went on. "You did well at Princeton. You were studious and you got good grades. However you kept to yourself the first two years and rarely dated—until you met Jamal.

"After he left you quit school for a year, not, as you told me at the casino, to just laze around, but to work. You worked two jobs, as a secretary for an insurance company during the day and as a waitress at night, to earn enough money to pay for your final year at school."

He took a deep breath. "You were desperate for money when you flung that twenty-thousand-dollar check back in my face, weren't you?"

There was a tremor in his voice that frightened her more than his usual harshness.

"Weren't you?" he asked again.

Katherine nodded.

"Yet you did it without even the slightest hesitation. I find that interesting."

"What has any of that to do with why you brought me here?"

"It tells me the type of woman you are and that I was wrong about you seven years ago when I thought you were a scheming little minx who wanted a bit of fun with a wealthy foreigner." He tapped long fingers against the table. "I must admit that when I saw you, you weren't what I expected. But even then I knew you weren't right for Jamal.

"My grandfather, who incidentally is half in love with you himself, agrees that a marriage between you and

Jamal would be disastrous. He has, however, suggested that you and I are suited."

Katherine's eyes narrowed in anger, but before she could speak Rashid said, "When I told him that you couldn't stand the sight of me he said I should make love to you and then see how you felt."

Silence ricocheted around the room. Katherine's face was frozen in shock.

"I should like very much to make love to you, Katherine. You see, I agree with my grandfather that I'd be better for you than Jamal. I love my brother but I know that he isn't man enough for a woman like you. You need a strong hand, someone who—"

"Perhaps you don't know Jamal as well as you think you do," she said as she raised one arched brow. "Perhaps he's more of a man than you think."

The color drained from Rashid's face. Before she could draw back, his hand shot out and grabbed her wrist. "Have you been having an affair with him?" His voice was a hiss of anger. "Damn you, Katherine Bishop, have you slept with my brother?"

For a moment she was tempted to lie. She wanted to strike out, to wound this man who looked at her as though he owned her. But when his hand tightened on her wrist, when he rasped again, "Have you?" she shook her head. Then, seeing the triumph in his eyes, she raised her chin and added, "Not yet."

"Then you will not. *You will not!*" He let go of her wrist and, obviously trying to calm himself, began to peel an orange. When he finished he put it on a clean plate and placed it before her.

"Marriage between an Arab and a foreigner is difficult, Katherine. I've seen this in my own family, between my grandparents. They've never divorced so it seems to me that there is the possibility they still love each other. But my grandmother found it impossible to adjust to life in Morocco."

He hesitated, then with a serious face said, "Have you ever looked around you in a restaurant here in Morocco? Haven't you noticed that usually there are no Arab women dining out? That except for one or two foreigners like yourself there are only men? Women simply don't go out socially with their husbands. If a woman must go out during the day, even with her husband or her father, she's veiled so that no other man may look upon her face or her form. She plays a passive role in society. If she must be seen, then she most certainly isn't heard. In her own home, when her husband entertains, she isn't present. She waits quietly in another room until the guests leave."

"Jamal wouldn't expect me to live like that."

"Jamal is a Moroccan, Katherine, as I am. Believe me when I tell you that it's exactly what he'd expect from his wife." He shook his head. "I don't think you could live that way. I can't imagine you ever playing a passive role in anything." His eyes were intent on hers. "However, I've brought you here to find out."

"What are you talking about?" She pressed her hands together to keep them from shaking.

"We're going to play make-believe for two weeks. We're going to pretend that you're a Moroccan wife, not the usual Moroccan wife, of course, but the wife of a fairly rich man. I've bought you clothes because it pleases me to see you dressed well. When we go out you'll be robed and veiled so that only your golden eyes will be visible. When I entertain here in my home you won't be present. However, should I wish you to make an appearance you will not speak unless you are spoken to and then you will answer what is asked and not express an opinion."

Katherine stared at him, her eyes widening in disbelief. "You can't do this!"

"Oh, but I can. Don't look so alarmed. I've told you—it will only be for two weeks. In that time I hope to convince you of two things." He reached out and captured one of her hands. "I hope to convince you that marriage to Jamal is quite impossible. And . . ."

Katherine waited.

"And I hope to convince you to become my mistress."

"Your mistress!" She pulled her hand away. Her face went white with shock. "You're insane," she said through trembling lips.

"Insane?" He shook his head. "No, Katherine, I'm not insane. But I am obsessed. I've been obsessed from the moment I saw you seven years ago."

He smiled a curiously gentle smile. "You were so convinced that you were unattractive, so painfully unsure of yourself, so awkward. I thought you were the loveliest woman I'd ever seen. You were like a flower just beginning to bud. You weren't even aware of what a beauty you were soon to be. But I knew, Katherine. I knew what a glory you'd be."

He studied her face. Then he broke the orange into sections and held one section to her lips. When, almost involuntarily, she opened her mouth to take it, he touched the inside of her lips with his index finger. It was an intimate gesture and she shivered.

"I knew of course that you were innocent," he went

on. "It was obvious in the way you moved, your shyness, the way you spoke. I was captivated. I wanted to take you away with me, to hide you from the world, from any eyes except my own. I wanted to teach you to love. I wanted to do everything to you that a man has ever done to a woman."

Katherine's hands tightened on the arm of the chair. She felt as though she couldn't breathe. She tried to look away from him and couldn't. Color crept to her cheeks and she was sure he could hear the beating of her heart. She was mesmerized by the sound of his voice, the intensity in his dark eyes. Her lip burned where he had touched her.

"Let me go," she whispered, and didn't know if she meant from this place or from the depths of his gaze.

"In two weeks," he said. "That's the time I've given myself. If in two weeks I haven't convinced you to give Jamal up, if in that time you haven't agreed to become my mistress, I'll take you back."

"I can ruin you."

"That's the chance I took when I brought you here."

The heat crushed down upon her, suffocating her so that she had to gasp for breath. It was too much. She couldn't bear it. Couldn't . . .

"What is it?" Rashid's voice seemed far away.

"I'm so . . ." She tried to open the neck of the caftan. "So warm. I—I can't breathe. . . ."

The room tilted and spun. She heard Rashid scrape back his chair. She felt herself being lifted in his arms.

"Fatima!" he shouted. "Fatima!"

An excited voice. The scurry of slippered feet. The opening of a door. Then she was laid gently down and in a minute she felt a cold cloth against her forehead.

"Katherine?" It was Rashid's voice. "Katherine, are you all right?"

Her eyelids fluttered open. "So warm," she whispered.

"It's my fault," he said. "I've frightened you."

"Let me go. Oh please, Rashid, let me go."

Dark desert eyes gazed down into hers. Slowly he shook his head. "I can't," he said. "I can't."

Chapter 8

LATE AFTERNOON SUN FILTERED IN THROUGH PARTIALLY closed blinds. Katherine stirred, then opened her eyes. The room was cooler. In the silence she heard the low and steady hum of the overhead fan. With a tentative hand she reached out and touched the satin sheet, remembering as she did that Rashid had laid her here. He had helped Fatima slip the caftan off and then, as gently as though she were a child, had bathed her face and arms and legs in cool rosewater.

With a sigh she rested her forearm across her eyes. She felt stronger now and knew that the weakness she'd felt earlier was because of the oppressive heat and because she hadn't eaten all day. Those things, coupled with the terrible fright of not knowing what was going to happen to her, had been too much.

But now she knew: Rashid wanted her to be his mistress. Mistress! That was crazy. Except for that one

kiss the night he'd brought her home from the casino
he'd never given any indication that he was the least bit
attracted to her. Yet a little while ago he had confessed
that he'd been obsessed with her for seven years.

Katherine lay for a long time, too emotionally exhausted to move, gazing around the room that at any
other time she would have admired. There was everything here a woman would want. The colors were her
colors. Had she the money she would have chosen the
same French perfumes Rashid had chosen. The clothes
were beautiful. Everything had been selected with taste
and thoughtfulness, even to the flowers and the
wrapped hard candies on the bedside table. She shook
her head. This was a dream; any moment she'd awaken
and find herself back in her apartment.

But it wasn't a dream, for at that moment Fatima
came in with a tray. She motioned for Katherine to sit
up and put the tray on her lap. There was a clear cool
soup, a fresh fruit salad and a glass of iced mint tea.

Fatima's face wrinkled in concentration. "Master say
eat or he come 'feet' you."

"And he said you didn't speak English!" Katherine
said with a slight grin. "Okay, Fatima, since I don't
want him anywhere near me I'll eat. I'll eat every time I
get a chance so that I'll be strong enough to get out of
here just as soon as I can figure out how."

She wasn't as frightened now as she had been. When
the plane landed and she'd seen the desolation she'd
thought that Rashid had meant to do away with her—if
not actually murder her, then just leave her out there
on the desert to die. But it seemed that wasn't what he
had in mind; his purpose in bringing her here was to get
her away from Jamal. That other—the part about her

being his mistress—was too ridiculous even to think about.

"When I do escape," she went on in a conversational tone as she bit into a piece of pineapple, "I'll go to the embassy and to the police and to anybody else who will listen and have your boss clapped in irons."

She took a sip of the iced tea. "Maybe they'll hang him upside down, Fatima, with a fifty-pound weight tied to his waist. Wouldn't that be lovely?"

Fatima's face wreathed in a smile and she bobbed her head.

"Or boiled in oil. I wonder if they still do that in Morocco. No—I've got it—we could have him staked out in the sand, over an anthill, and have a whole troop of camels tromp on him. Then—"

"And you call me a barbarian!" Rashid said from the doorway.

Katherine looked up, startled. She'd been so caught up in the sheer pleasure of all the things she'd do to him when she got a chance that she hadn't heard him.

"Go on," he said. "I didn't know you had such a vivid imagination. I'm fascinated. I particularly liked the part about staking me out on the sand and having a troop of camels run over me." He looked down at her tray. "Finish your salad," he ordered. "It might improve your disposition."

He waited until she finished, then said something to Fatima who quickly took the tray off Katherine's lap. Bobbing her head the woman said, *"Ma'al salama."*

"Ṭusba al khair," Rashid answered.

"What did she say?" Katherine asked when the woman bowed herself out.

"She said *ma'al salama*, peace be with you, and I

responded *tusba al khair,* which is our evening good-bye. Would you like me to teach you some Arabic?"

"No, I would not!"

"I know this has all been a great shock to you, Katherine, and I'm sorry. I wish we could have gotten you here in a more civilized way. I suppose that I'm not a civilized man after all. But I do keep my promises. I've promised that if you still wish to return to Rabat in two weeks I'll fly you back. If the authorities don't tie me to a stake and let a troop of camels run over me I'll also promise never to see you again."

She pulled the sheet up to her chin. "And not to interfere with Jamal and me—with our wedding plans?"

Angry desert eyes burned into hers. But finally he nodded and said, "I promise."

"It won't do you any good, Rashid, keeping me here like this. I'll never agree to give up Jamal. But even if I did, the thought of becoming your mistress is—"

In two strides he crossed the room and stood looking down at her. "Is what?" he said softly.

"Ludicrous!"

"Is it really? I wonder." He touched her face, grasping her chin when she tried to jerk away. He ran his thumb across her lips. Then, before she could squirm away, he kissed her, pinning down the arms that were under the satin sheet so that she couldn't move against him.

Katherine lay still, her lips compressed and tight because she knew that was the only way she could fight him. She felt his hands tighten on her arms as his lips pressed against her. He nipped the corners of her mouth, her lips, and when she cried out in protest he plunged his tongue in her mouth and she heard him gasp with pleasure.

Strong hands kept her pinned while his warm and savage mouth ravaged her. He nibbled at the inside of her lips, soothed them with his tongue, then sucked at her lower lip as though it were a ripe strawberry.

Suddenly he let go of her hands and, slipping an arm under her shoulders, drew her closer. With the other hand he soothed her hair back from her face, caressing her forehead, her cheeks, her throat. All the while he kissed her. Kissed her until something insidious and terrible began to happen to her body.

She softened, yielding even as she whimpered in protest.

"Katherine." He whispered her name against her lips.

"No!"

With a small sigh he pushed a strand of hair back from her face and released her. "Why do you deny what we both know?" he asked. "Why do you pretend there's nothing between us? You knew there was something the night we went to the casino. You knew it when we danced and later when we kissed."

His hand moved down her face to her throat, and almost to himself he said, "How fair you are. How delicate your skin is against the darkness of my hand." His eyes were warm, his nostrils fluted with desire. "I don't think you love Jamal, Katherine. I don't think you intended to become engaged to him. I saw the way you looked the night he gave you the gold marriage belt. You were appalled; you didn't want to take it.

Then you looked at me and saw my anger. I think you accepted the belt to get back at me for separating the two of you seven years ago."

"That's not true!"

"I hurt you seven years ago—now you're trying to hurt me." His hands moved to her shoulders. "It's time for the hurting to stop, Katherine. It's time for the loving to begin."

"No!" Her voice was a low hiss of protest. Her golden eyes narrowed to tiger slits and she pulled away from him. "Loving! How can you even use that word?"

She sat up and pulled the sheet closer around her body. "There'll never be a time for loving, Rashid. Not for us. I'm going to marry Jamal and there isn't a thing you can do about it. You've promised to take me back to Rabat in two weeks. I can only hope you'll honor that promise. But let me tell you right now that whether you keep me here for two weeks or two years or two decades, nothing will ever change the way I feel about you." She took a deep breath. "I despise you. I'll never understand how you and Jamal could be brothers. He's dear and kind and gentle and you're—"

He leaned over her, an arm on either side of her body. "I'm what, Katherine?"

"You're a despicable brute. You're a man who takes what he wants and who doesn't care who gets hurt in the process. You're a barbarian, Rashid, and I can't stand the sight of you."

He let her go. His face was pale, his lips compressed and angry. At the door he turned and said, "I don't know why the hell I brought you here. You're bad-tempered, spiteful and impossible. But as long as you *are* here you'll do what I tell you to do. For the next two weeks you'll behave as I tell you to behave and you'll dress as I tell you to dress."

"I won't!" she shouted.

"Yes, you will!" he shouted back.

He stood there, legs apart, hands clenched at his sides, and for a moment Katherine was afraid he was going to come back. Then with a low curse he turned on his heel and went out, slamming the door behind him.

The veil tickled Katherine's nose. She experimented with small puffs of breath, trying to blow it away from her face.

She'd never felt so wrapped up, so *swathed* in clothing from the top of her head where the cloth had been wrapped low over her forehead to cover her hair, down to her ankles. The veil was fastened just below her eyes.

All that was visible were her golden eyes. She could have been a Moroccan woman getting ready to go out with her husband. But no, she thought angrily as she gazed at herself in the mirror, not my husband, my captor.

She'd been here now for three days. This morning Rashid had instructed Fatima to dress her for leaving the house. When the woman led her into the living room Rashid looked at her with approval.

"Now you look like a proper Moroccan woman," he said with a slight smile. "See that you behave like one." He nodded to Fatima and when she left the room he said to Katherine, "It's a strange thing. Perhaps it's because I know what a lovely body is hidden under your robe and what a beautiful face lies behind the veil, but you're even more desirable now. There's a mysterious sexuality in your eyes that I don't think you're even aware of. You excite me, Katherine. You excite me more than any woman I've ever known."

He moved so close that she could feel his breath on her face. "I want to rip your robe off and kiss every fragrant and lovely inch of you. I want . . ." His nostrils flared. He took a deep shaking breath. "But I won't," he said in a soft voice. "I won't, because when we make love I want you to want me as much as I want you."

"Then you'll wait forever," she snapped.

A muscle jumped in his cheek. "We'll see." He put a hand on her shoulder. "Now come, I want to show you my oasis."

His oasis. His land, his people, his camels, his horses. His captive.

Tall palms grew alongside the spring-fed river. There were tamarisk trees, a sprinkling of flowers and scrubby shrubs. Beyond lay the endless vastness of the Sahara.

As they moved along Katherine almost forgot the oppressive heat and began to watch the people around her, people who were as curious about her as she was about them.

"Do you feel all right?" Rashid asked. "The temperature is well over a hundred today. Sometimes it gets up to a hundred and thirty-five. It isn't too much for you?"

"No, but I can't understand why of all the places in the world you selected this godforsaken one to build a home."

"I like the desert. It's as simple and as complicated as that. I have a home in Rabat and an apartment in Paris, but this is the place I like best. There's something about it—the heat of the desert days, the cool of the nights. I like the challenge, the strength it takes for these people to survive."

"They're Berbers?"

He nodded. "The Greeks and the Romans called them Barbarians." He laughed. "A word you're familiar with, of course. They've always been a fighting race. They're fiercely independent and tough; some of them are nomads who wander from place to place in the desert, completely independent of any form of government. But most of them, like these people, settle in village communities."

"Why do the women have tatoos?"

"To indicate their tribe, the region they're from. They use some kind of vegetable dye and insert it under the skin with needles."

"My God! Don't they get an infection?"

"I suppose they do from time to time. But they seem to survive; they've been doing it for centuries." He gestured back beyond the house. "That's where they live," he said. "They still construct their houses with bricks made of mud and straw." He took her arm. "Come along, I want to show you the stables."

The stables had been built under a group of tall palm trees, and as they approached Katherine saw a line of stalls and heads poked out of the half-doors. The animals whinnied when they caught sight of Rashid. He stopped at the first stall to rub the horse's nose. "This is Desert Witch," he said as he unfastened the bottom door. "Come and have a look at her foal. He's a week old today. Isn't he a beauty? I've named him Calafia."

The colt was black, with white stockings on his forelegs, sleek and muscled, eyes alert, ears perked.

"Aren't you beautiful!" Katherine said as she reached to scratch behind his ears, forgetting for a moment that she didn't want to be here.

"You like horses?"

"Oh yes."

"Do you ride?"

"I used to. I haven't since I've been in Morocco."

"Then we'll go riding in the desert some evening when it's cool."

Katherine glanced up at him, her eyes as veiled as her face before she turned back to the colt.

After a few minutes Rashid said, "You can see him again tomorrow." He took her arm, led her to the next stall and said, "This is Jezebel. She's almost ready to foal." He rubbed the horse's head and moved on, calling each horse by name: Sultan, who had fathered Calafia; Intrepid, a handsome gray; and Dorado, a golden two-year-old.

Finally he led Katherine past the stables to a corral. He gave a low whistle and the most beautiful horse Katherine had ever seen galloped up to the fence.

"Hello, boy," Rashid said as he leaned over the rail to rub the stallion's nose. "This is Corsair," he told Katherine, "my prize stallion. I think he's the most beautiful horse in Morocco."

"He's magnificent!" As much as Katherine hated to show enthusiasm for anything that belonged to Rashid, she simply couldn't help herself. She'd never seen an animal like this one. He was big and his lines were regal and perfect, but it was his color that made her gasp in admiration. He was a sleek bronze, with a coat so fine it looked as though he had been varnished.

"Oh, you're beautiful," Katherine said as she

stepped up on one of the rungs of the corral fence and reached out to stroke the sleek nose.

"Be careful," Rashid cautioned as the stallion raised its head, shying away.

"It's this robe," Katherine said. "All this material flapping in his face. It would be all right if I had on blue jeans and a shirt. How can women stand to go around dressed like this?"

"They dress that way because they're modest," Rashid said smoothly. "Too modest to parade their faces and figures to the whole world."

"Oh for—!" Katherine's yellow eyes spit fire as, hands on her hips, she glared at him. "That's chauvinistic garbage. You Arabs have kept these poor women under your thumbs for years. You keep them home all covered up while you go out to ogle a woman not half as pretty do a belly dance."

"A belly dancer is a professional woman who expects to be looked at. We respect our wives too much to expose them to anything like that."

"Wives is right. *Four* wives!"

"There are not too many Moroccans who have four." He grinned at her. "Wives are expensive. Whatever you buy for one you must buy for the other. And you must not shower all of your affection on one, but spread it equally among the four so none will be jealous. If you visit Zohra on Monday then you must visit Latifa on Tuesday, Hadidsha on Wednesday and Jima on Thursday."

"That's terrible!"

"Terrible? It's wonderful!" He laughed. "A man needs variety. He doesn't want a diet of lamb and rice four times a week."

"Oh!" Katherine was so angry she wanted to scream. But before she could say anything else Rashid said, "Katherine, I'm teasing. There are very few multiple marriages anymore. It's mostly a simple matter of economics—it's only the rich who can afford four wives."

"You're rich."

"Not rich, just fairly well off."

"You could have four wives."

"Yes, I suppose I could." He stepped closer to her. "But I don't have any, not even one. I don't want a wife. I only want a—"

"A mistress."

"I only want you." Eyes as black as night gazed down into hers. "I only want you," he said again, "any way I can get you."

Katherine stared up at him. "Jamal is your brother," she said in an even voice. "You've told me that you've always taken care of him, that you've been brother, father and friend. I can't believe you want to destroy all that, that you'd sacrifice your relationship with him this way."

She put her hand on his arm. "Let me go, Rashid. I promise you that if you do we can forget this ever happened. I won't tell Jamal. I won't tell anybody. But you can't go on with this charade. You can't do this to me—you mustn't do it to Jamal."

For one long moment Rashid looked down into her eyes. "You're a witch," he said at last. "You bewitched Jamal and now you've bewitched me. I wish neither of us had ever set eyes on you."

"Oh, so do I," Katherine said as she turned away. "So do I."

Chapter 9

MOONLIGHT LAY IN A GOLDEN PATH ACROSS THE ROUND
bed. Katherine couldn't sleep, so finally she got up and
went to stand out on the balcony overlooking the
gardens.

Everything was hauntingly quiet. The palm trees cast
strange shadows, their fronds reflecting fingerlike
movements against the desert sky. Beyond the oasis she
could see the dunes, like cresting waves, shimmering in
the moonlight. There was a scent in the air tonight, not
the familiar scent of jasmine or roses, but a stronger,
headier smell. A smell of animals and people and
earth.

She leaned against the railing. The pale mauve
nightgown, stirred by the breeze, caressed her warm
skin. With a sigh she brushed the wheat-gold hair back
from her face. It was hard to be angry on a night as soft
as this.

Below in the garden something moved and she retreated into the shadows. Then, with another restless sigh she went to the bed, propping the pillows behind her back. She'd been here four days now. Rashid had said he'd release her in two weeks. If he kept his word . . .

There was a light tap on the door. Before she could speak the doorknob turned and Rashid, wearing a loose white djellaba, stood in a shaft of light from the corridor.

"I saw you from your balcony," he said. "I was down in the garden. Are you all right?"

Katherine pulled the satin sheet up, trying to cover herself. "Yes, yes, I'm all right."

For a long moment he looked at her. Then he came in, closing the door behind him, and crossed the room to her bed.

Her heart thudded against her ribcage. "What do you want?" she managed to say.

"I want a woman who has bewitched me," he murmured. "A woman I've dreamed about for seven long years."

She felt choked with fear but managed to lift her chin and say, in what she hoped was a calm voice, "Will you please leave?"

He shook his head, and with a low groan pulled her into his arms, his face against hers, one arm around her shoulders, the other hand against her hair. "I love your hair," he whispered, rubbing a strand of it between his fingers. "I love the silk of it, the scent of it." He touched her throat with his lips. "The scent of you."

"No!" She tried to struggle out of his arms.

"Your skin is like silk," he said with his lips still

against her throat. "Are you like this all over? Oh God, Katherine, you feel so good."

He flung the satin sheet back and, lying down beside her, pulled her into his arms. When she cried out and struggled against him, he pressed her even closer so that the whole length of his body was outlined to hers. And she knew he wore nothing under the djellaba.

Almost frantic with fear, Katherine tried to push him away, but before she could move or speak his mouth descended on hers and his probing tongue thrust its way into her mouth as his arms tightened around her protesting body.

"I love to taste you," he whispered. "I love to feel you tremble as you're trembling now." He kissed her temple, then traced a line of kisses down to her lips again, softly teasing, kissing the corners, taking her lower lip between his teeth to run his tongue back and forth across it.

"Stop it!" With all her strength Katherine pushed him away. The mauve gown ripped, exposing her breasts.

"You're so beautiful. How can you be so beautiful?" He pulled her back into his arms, holding her face against his. "Don't tremble so," he whispered as his lips moved down the line of her jaw to kiss her ear. When still she struggled he gently nipped the lobe before he moved down to her throat.

"I can feel the beat of your heart," he said and put his lips against the frantic pulse. His hands gentled her body with caresses. "Shhh," he soothed. "Shhh," as he began to stroke her breasts.

"No!" She tried to twist free. "I won't let you!" She grasped his wrists and pushed him away from her, then tried to roll away. But he pulled her back and held her, his body half over hers, and with his mouth against her breasts reached out to flick the nearest with his tongue.

She struck out and he grasped her wrists with one strong hand and held them pinned against the satin pillow above her head as with tender persistence he took a nipple in his mouth, rolling his tongue around it, sucking it to a taut peak before he scraped his teeth against it.

Katherine cried out in anger, writhing against the body that lay half over hers, then stopped when she heard his gasp of pleasure, knowing she was exciting him even more. She stopped and lay still, hands clenched, trying with every bit of will she possessed to hold her body still, to keep silent against the assault.

Trying—even when his free hand caressed her other breast, rolling the nipple between his thumb and forefinger, teasing the hard peak while his mouth, his relentless mouth, suckled the other.

"Don't!" The word was a frenzied cry in the stillness of the room. "Oh please, please don't. Oh please, Rashid, Rashid."

"Lie still, darling," he whispered against her skin before his lips closed around the tender tip again.

She couldn't stand this. Couldn't . . . could not bear this. Her body was on fire . . . on fire with longing. She hated him. She couldn't stand this. Oh God, she wanted him. Wanted him.

"I hate you," she whispered. "Oh stop. Oh please stop. Rashid, oh Rashid."

He moved up her body to claim her lips, to kiss away her words of hate. When he let go of her wrists she grasped his shoulders to thrust him away. And could not. Could not as her traitorous mouth answered his kiss with a hunger as urgent as his own. She was lost in a heaven of desire, her body quivering with need.

His lips cut a path of flame down her throat, nibbling the sensitive skin, moving again to her breasts while his strong dark hands caressed her trembling body. When the gown got in his way he ripped it off so that Katherine lay naked against him. Freely now he stroked the lines of her hips, the slight roundness of her stomach, her smooth white thighs.

His hand was warm and alive against her skin, sending stabs of electric feeling everywhere it touched. He kissed the tender line between belly and thigh, then ran his tongue across her skin as his hand moved to the apex of her thighs.

"No!" With one great surge of effort Katherine wrenched his hand away.

"You want me," he said in a choked voice. "You want me just as much as I want you."

"I don't. I don't." She rolled her head from side to side in an agony of denial and shame. "I don't!" she cried again.

His hand reached out to touch her breast and she struck it away. She was crying now, crying with anger and hate and longing.

"Someday I won't let you stop me," Rashid declared. "Someday I'll do everything to you that I want to do. I'll make you beg me not to stop."

With a cry of anger he drew her to him again, his mouth hard and demanding against hers now. When her nails dug into his shoulders he grasped her wrists. "Damn you," he whispered against her throat. "Damn you."

Now his mouth burned a line of fire across her breasts and down her body, biting with sharp white teeth, then soothing with his tongue. Suddenly he let go of her wrists and, thrusting her legs apart, nipped her inner thigh so hard she gasped in pain.

"This is where I'd tattoo you if you were mine," he threatened with his lips against her skin. "This is where I'd put my mark so that if any man ever tried to touch you he'd know you belonged to my tribe, that you were my woman."

Katherine was frightened, frightened by the intensity in his voice and by feelings and urgencies in her own body. "Let me go," she pleaded, and began to cry again.

Rashid took a long shuddering breath. Then he let her go and his hands began to soothe the place he had hurt. After a while he put a hand on her bare hip and in a gentle voice said, "Don't cry, Katherine." Then he pulled the sheet over her and quietly left the room.

She cried for a long time, then finally, as exhausted as she had ever been in her life, drifted into a troubled restless sleep.

The next morning she began to plan her escape.

After she finished the breakfast Fatima brought her, she soaked for a long time in the deep turquoise bathtub. There were bruises on her wrists and a small blue mark where Rashid had nipped her inner thigh. Closing her eyes, she let herself drift back into the memory of the night.

She knew, though she hated to admit it, that she had never responded to Jamal in the way that she had responded to Rashid. Jamal's kisses were soothing and pleasant, but Rashid's kisses had stirred her to a depth of passion she had not even dreamed possible.

Oh damn, she thought, leaning her head back against the tub, feeling a flush of shame and remembered passion. Damn! Everything was such a mess. Rashid had been right last night when he told her that she'd accepted the gold marriage belt only to spite him. She really hadn't wanted to become engaged to Jamal. She didn't want to marry him. He was sweet and dear and she was fond of him, but deep in her heart she knew she didn't love him. She'd been foolish to try to recapture those wonderful springtime days at Princeton. Those days were gone; she was a woman now.

That morning, when she was dressed and veiled, she and Fatima walked around the oasis. There were two small shops, one that sold canned goods and staples, another that sold miscellaneous things like candles, cloth, needles and thread, rope and teapots. A water seller, brass cups jingling around his neck, wandered through the small center plaza.

Rashid was away for the day. He had left a note saying that he didn't expect to return until quite late and that she should dine without him. "I'm sorry if I hurt you last night," the note read. "When we have settled down a bit we can discuss this thing that is between us. Do not deny that there is something between us, my darling Katherine."

Her face flamed. Her determination to get as far away from Rashid as she could strengthened. Her gaze roamed the oasis. There were no guards, and except for the curious stares of the women and children it appeared that there was only Fatima to watch her. She looked back towards the stables, then at the jeep still parked in the open garage.

When the children came closer she smiled at them. A little boy tossed a ball to her. She tossed it back, edging toward the jeep. When the boy threw the ball she purposely missed it, letting it roll close enough to the jeep so that she could glance in at the dashboard. The keys were in the ignition.

Grinning behind her veil, barely able to suppress her excitement, Katherine tossed the ball back to the boy. Tonight, she thought, I'm going to escape tonight while Rashid is gone. I can be in Erfoud by the time he returns.

The wind began to blow late that afternoon. Clouds scudded and the sky darkened. Katherine's spirits rose when people ran for cover. It was perfect; she'd never have another opportunity like this. By tonight everyone would be indoors. All she had to do was slip unnoticed out of the house and get to the jeep. Then she'd follow the same road they'd taken to come here, watch for the turnoff to Erfoud and once there go to the police and ask for their protection.

She was so excited she could barely eat the dinner Fatima brought to her room. Twice she faked a yawn. Finally she put her hands under her head and closed her eyes, pretending to sleep. Fatima nodded. She turned back the bed and, bowing to Katherine, prepared to leave. For one fleeting moment Katherine felt an inexplicable pang of regret. "Goodbye," she said, "Goodbye, Fatima."

The Berber woman looked puzzled, then smiled her shy smile and bowed herself out the door.

Katherine waited until the house was quiet. Finally, the lights dim and the curtains drawn, she dressed in a dark blue djellaba and bound her hair in a shawl-type scarf. She had no suitcase so she emptied the makeup case and inside it she put a few pieces of underwear, a nightgown, hairbrush, toothbrush, a bar of scented soap, a mirror and lipstick. Then, because she didn't know how long a drive it would be to Erfoud, she put an orange and a few hard candies in her pocket.

For one last time she looked around the bedroom. Trying to pretend that what she felt was not a stab of pain, she stepped into the darkened corridor and moved silently through the house. The only sound she heard was the whistling of the wind in the palm trees.

She took a deep breath and stepped outside, surprised at how strong the wind was and at the fine particles of sand that stung her face.

Quickly she ran across the yard to the open garage, slid into the driver's seat, and fumbled on the dashboard for the keys. Praise Allah, she thought, grinning to herself, they were still there. She turned the key, struggled for a minute trying to find reverse, then with a screech of tires backed the jeep out, threw it into first and headed for the road.

When Katherine turned the headlights on, she was surprised to see how dark it was. Sand, drifting like snow, narrowed the already narrow private road, and pinged against the windshield, making it almost impossible to see. She turned on the windshield wipers. They worked for a few minutes, then became clogged with sand.

For the first time since she had left Rashid's oasis Katherine felt a stab of fear. She was so totally alone here in this small enclosed space, alone in a world of swirling sand. She glanced at her watch and by the light on the dashboard saw that forty-five minutes had passed. She should have reached the main road ten minutes ago.

Slowing the car to a crawl, she felt the pull of the tires against the deepening sand. The car slowed, grunted forward, then stopped. Katherine put it in reverse and heard the wheels spin. She tried turning to her left, then to her right, but it wouldn't budge. As frustrated as she was frightened now, she turned the motor off. There was nothing she could do but stay where she was until morning, when she would be able to see the road.

Sand crept in between the plastic visors, grit drifted around her. She pulled the head covering around her face and, arms crossed over her chest, settled back in the seat and tried to relax. In the morning, she told herself as she closed her eyes, in the morning I'll be able to see the road.

But there was no road. There was only a vast sea of sand stretching as far as Katherine could see. She had driven off the road the night before and hadn't even known it. She could be five miles—even ten—out in the desert.

Her hands tightened on the steering wheel as she looked around her, trying to stay calm, trying to quell her growing panic.

The wind had stopped. The inside of the jeep was an inferno of heat. Finally, because she knew she couldn't stay here forever, she tried to open the door. She shoved as hard as she could, her heart beating fast in fear, but it wouldn't open. She began to tear at the visor on her side, ripping it from the snaps that held it. When it came loose she pulled herself up out of the jeep. Braced there on the side, she looked around her. There was nothing—not a bird, a tree, a shrub— nothing except an endless expanse of sand.

She reached back in the jeep and got the makeup case, then lowered herself to the sand. The jeep was stuck in sand halfway up to the doors. Even if she had a shovel she doubted she'd be able to dig it out.

She had no choice; she had to return to Rashid's oasis. But in which direction should she go? She looked around her, bewildered. Last night she'd driven for more than forty-five minutes. She knew now with a terrible certainty that for part of that time she hadn't been on the road but headed straight out into the desert.

Her hand tightened around the makeup case as she tried to fight back her growing panic. Finally, taking a deep breath, she started away from the jeep, heading in the direction she thought she had come.

The desert was an endless solitude of heat and sunscorched sand shimmering in a sea of blinding light. Katherine bound up her hair, pulling the cloth low over her forehead to protect her face from the painful rays of the sun. Glancing at her wristwatch she saw that it was only nine o'clock. The temperature already was over a hundred degrees. What would it be like at noon?

Nervously she unwrapped a hard candy and put it in her mouth. She'd wait and eat the orange when she could no longer bear the growing thirst. Two hours later she had to have it.

She peeled it carefully, conserving the skin to eat later. Just in case, she told herself. Just in case. She ate slowly, biting into each section so as not to lose one sweet drop of juice, rolling each bite around on her tongue, chewing it slowly. Although she'd told herself she'd eat only half of it now she couldn't stop until she'd finished. But she still had the skin; there'd be some juice in that. Everything would be all right if she just kept going.

By noon the desert was a hell of heat. Through the thin soles of the jeweled slippers Katherine's feet burned. Sweat trickled down her body. When she began to feel dizzy she ate the orange skins. When they were gone she kept fingering the hard candies, but every time she reached for one she told herself, wait, wait. You'll need them later.

They'd be serving lunch at Rashid's now. Cool Perrier water with a twist of lime, clear soup, a leafy-green salad with that sharp touch of vinegar she liked. She licked her lips and put a hard candy in her mouth.

How long could people live in this heat? she wondered. Even people who were used to it? Camels lived a long time, but they had all that water stored in their bodies and thick hair to keep them cool. Don't think about cool. Don't think about water.

"Wish I were a camel, wish I were a camel," she chanted. "Wish I—" Suddenly she stopped. Ahead of her, shining in the sun, she saw a pool of water. With one joyous cry she lifted her skirt and ran toward it, mumbling in frustration because it was further than she thought, crying aloud when it disappeared before her eyes.

"Idiot!" she mumbled. "Everybody knows about

mirages. Only a fool goes running toward one." She put another hard candy in her mouth.

She didn't think that anything would save her now but she was determined to go on. Rashid would be looking for her. He would never find her in this vast open space, but she knew he would try. It seemed strange that of all the men in the world he was the one she thought of now. If it hadn't been for him she'd still be back in Rabat, sitting at her desk in her lovely air-conditioned office. Rashid had tricked her. He had kidnapped her and tried to seduce her, not because he cared for her but because he didn't want Jamal to marry her. She hated him, but she trusted his strength. If anybody could find her he could.

Katherine licked her dry lips and reached for another hard candy. One pocket was empty. She reached in the other one. Empty! There were no more candies!

"It's okay, okay," she told herself. "Take it easy. You're going to be all right if you just keep going."

The sand tilted. Katherine stumbled and fell to her knees. She stayed that way for a little while. "Please God," she mumbled. "Please Allah. Don't let me die out here. Give me the strength to go on. Let Rashid find me. Please let him find me."

Eyes closed, she willed herself to her feet and went on, on through the scorching, shimmering sea of sand. On while the sun seared down through her scalp to her brain, while the sweat rolled off her body and her lips cracked and bled. One step at a time, she told herself. One step at a time.

When she saw, through the glare of sun and sand, the pond of water she smiled through swollen lips. "Can't fool me this time. Fool all of the people some of the time and some . . . but can't fool me again." She giggled. "Hey," she said, "there are even some trees around this mirage. How's that for seeing things? How's . . . ?"

The scene swam before her eyes, tipped and swayed as she struggled forward. Closer, ever closer, until at last she saw that it wasn't a mirage after all, that there really were trees. And a pool of water.

Water! Dry sobs racked her parched throat as she staggered toward it. Stumbling across the rocks that led to the shaded pool, she threw herself down on her stomach and put her face in the water, almost hysterical with relief. She drank, she splashed it on her face, then drank again. Finally she rolled over on the rocks, in the shade of the trees, and went to sleep.

Chapter 10

IT WAS STILL DAYLIGHT WHEN KATHERINE WOKE. SHE looked around her, trying to remember where she was. When she sat up she still felt dizzy, but better. She took the covering off her head, then stood up, stripped out of her djellaba and went to the pool.

The cool water felt wonderful against her skin. She scooped it up in her hands, drinking her fill again, then lay down in it so that water covered her body.

She stayed like that for a long time and when she got out picked a handful of dates, wondering idly how long a person could live on dates and water. But it was a rhetorical wondering, not a fearful one. She was clean and cool; her thirst had been slaked, her hunger satisfied. Nothing terrible was going to happen to her—at least not right away.

Far out on the desert she saw a small cloud of dust. A whirlwind? she wondered. Another storm? She went to the edge of the oasis, her hand shading her eyes, and watched the cloud come closer. When she realized it was a horse and rider she began to wave.

"Here!" she cried. "Here!" Even though she knew she was too far away to be heard.

At last she saw that the man was covered by a burnoose and that the horse was the color of bronze. She knew it was Corsair. Rashid had found her.

He saw her wave and raised his arm, but rather than slowing Corsair he urged the horse on faster, bringing the huge animal up short as he leapt off and ran to Katherine.

Before she could speak Rashid grabbed her and began to shake her. "Are you all right?" he cried. "My God, Katherine. I never thought I'd find you again."

Still damp strands of hair flew about her face as he shook her.

"Let me go," she protested, trying to break free.

But he clasped her to him, holding her so tightly she couldn't breathe. "You could have died out there," he said over and over again, "It's a miracle you didn't." He held her away from him. "Are you sure you're all right? God, your skin is on fire."

He pulled her back into his arms again. The rough material of his burnoose scratched her and when she flinched he let go and looked at her. For the first time he became aware of what she was wearing.

In the excitement of seeing Rashid, she'd forgotten that she'd taken off the caftan and was wearing only the lace bra and skimpy satin panties. With a gasp of embarrassment she tried to pull away from him so that she could cover herself.

Rashid tightened his grip as his eyes slowly raked her.

"You're beautiful," he said at last. Then he pulled her into his arms again and his mouth found hers in a kiss that totally possessed and enveloped her.

"I was so afraid," he whispered against her lips. "When I found the jeep . . ." His voice broke. "Why did you run away like that? Out into the desert? Do you hate me that much, Katherine?"

"Rashid, please . . ."

"Damn you! Damn you for making me want you like I do." He pulled her into his arms and again his mouth covered hers. With a strangled cry he swept her off her feet and carried her to a shady spot under the palms. He put her down and before she could even speak he ripped his burnoose off and tossed it aside. Reaching for her he forced her down on the rough material.

"I've waited too long," he said in a hoarse voice. His nostrils flared with desire. "Too long."

"No! No, don't!" Katherine cried, but his mouth covered hers, taking the words, taking her breath. When she struggled beneath him, his hand fastened on the lace bra, sliding it off as he leaned to kiss her breasts. Roughly, feverishly, he scraped the tender nipples with his tongue and his teeth, then with a low cry pulled her underpants down over her hips.

Katherine struck him a glancing blow on the side of his face that made him curse in anger. He drew back, out of the range of her fists, swiftly disrobed and caught her to him.

Every inch of their naked bodies touched. He tangled his fingers in her golden hair, holding her head while his mouth sought hers. His hand slid down her body to her belly, her hips, the silken triangle.

"I've wanted to touch you like this from the moment I saw you seven years ago," he murmured against her lips. "And that night at Rabat, when you were all white and gold and so indescribably beautiful. Oh God, Katherine, I've wanted you for such a long time."

His mouth sought hers, hard and hurting, his teeth assaulting the corners of her mouth with sharp little nips before he forced her mouth open to ravage it with his tongue.

When she tried to push him away the muscles of his shoulders tensed. His hard-as-steel legs tightened around her. She could feel the heat of his breath against her skin, the quick tortured breathing while he held her and whispered, "I want you. I want you," and then thrust himself into her.

Katherine cried out, fists flailing against him until he pinned her wrists to the ground, plunging again into her tender flesh.

"Oh, the feel of you," he cried. "The sweet warm feel of you."

His movements quickened and when Katherine cried out against the onslaught his mouth found hers again, more gently this time, and the hands that held her soothed and caressed. His body moved against hers, slower, deeper, enveloping her in his maleness.

Deep within her something stirred. She fought, tightening her body, trying to hold herself aloof, trying to deny the insidious warmth that grew and spread.

"I hate you," she whispered. "Oh God, how I hate you. How I—"

He took her words into his mouth. When his tongue

touched hers his movements quickened. She felt him grow taut, heard the sharp intake of his breath. Then, with a cry that was part joy and part anguish, his body was still and he whispered her name against her lips.

For a long time he didn't speak. He lay, his body covering hers, his face lost in the tangle of her hair. When finally he stirred he turned his face and said, "I'm sorry. . . ." With infinite tenderness he traced the line of her face, pushing the hair back from her eyes.

"Will you let me go, please?" Katherine kept her voice as cold as ice, but she couldn't meet Rashid's eyes.

"No, I won't let you go." He kissed her neck. "Now be still and let me rest."

He slept, and after a while, exhausted by all that had happened, Katherine did too. Slept to dream of hot summer afternoons and chocolate ice cream. She was at her grandfather's house in Portland, sitting bare-legged on the old horsehair sofa. It prickled her legs and she squirmed. The ice cream disappeared before she could put it in her mouth. She felt frustrated and angry so she lay back on the sofa, trying not to mind the prickles. She was warm, but it wasn't an unpleasant warm. She stretched a lazy cat stretch. Ummm . . . a lovely tide of delicious feeling suffused her body. She moved against it and felt a flush of pleasure so intense that she gave a small murmur of surprise. Another tentative movement brought an even greater feeling of pleasure, a sensual—

Her eyes flew open and above her, his face only inches from hers, she saw Rashid.

"What . . . ?"

As he kissed her, his tongue slipped into her mouth

and she shivered, still half asleep, unable to fight this strange reality. This reality of him inside her, moving slowly against her body as his tongue caressed the lips that had been swollen by the sun and bruised by his roughness.

When his lips left hers to travel down her throat she gave a small moan of protest.

"Shhh," he murmured against her skin as his tongue touched one peaked nipple, circling it slowly before he took it in his mouth. All the while he moved against her, growing, warming, exciting.

Katherine's body arched against his. "Don't," she protested. "Don't."

But his lips persisted, caressing first one then the other breast with his lips and his silken tongue, tenderly now as though trying to kiss away the hurt he'd inflicted before. When his mouth found hers again his hands slipped under her shoulders to draw her closer as the slow, torturous movements quickened.

Katherine had never felt like this, never felt this terrible reaching, this demand for fulfillment. Her body quivered with passion, her fingers tightened in his hair and she cried his name as she pressed close to him.

"Rashid," she murmured against his skin. "Rashid."

"Look at me," he commanded, and when she did she saw the passion in his dark desert eyes. "Know that I am Rashid Ben Hasir and that you belong to me," he said.

"No!" Katherine's hands tightened on his back. Her nails raked his skin and he gasped in pain. "I don't belong to you," she cried, even as her body lifted to his and the hands that had wounded moved down his back to press him closer.

His mouth found hers and his body plunged against her. It was too much. Past bearing. She closed her eyes and tasted the skin of his shoulder, rubbed her face against the matted hair of his chest, wanting to get closer and closer still to this man, this man with the dark desert eyes.

His hands tightened on her as he whispered her name against her lips and suddenly, with a cry, her body exploded into a thousand shimmering pieces of golden light. Up and up and up into the blueness of the sky, into the brightness of the sun that blinded her, lifted her, made her cry his name over and over as his arms tightened around her and he whispered her name triumphantly against her mouth.

As twilight settled over the oasis Rashid rose and carried Katherine to the pool. The world was still and deserted. They were alone, two people in the vastness of this quiet place as the sun streaked the sky with vermilion, yellow and turquoise, and the coming evening cast shadows on the shifting sands.

The fading sunlight struck Rashid's naked body, making his dark skin glow as he bent to catch the drops of water off Katherine's peaked pink breasts, to lap with a gentle tongue the sweetness of the water and of her.

Too tired to protest, bewildered by all that had happened to her in the last twenty-four hours, she stood within the circle of his arms and let him do what he would with her.

When finally he led her out of the pool, he watered Corsair. Then he made a bed of fronds and moss under the palm trees, covered over with his burnoose.

"Come," he said in a gentle voice. And when she did he lay down beside her, and pulling her against his chest held her until she slept.

Katherine Bishop. Rashid smiled as he brushed his chin against her hair. What made her different from all other women? What special magic did she have that made him want her so?

He remembered how she looked the first time he had seen her, a gangly, awkward, unsure-of-herself woman, wearing heavy clothes to hide her thinness and low-heeled shoes to minimize her height.

When Jamal had written him about this young American he was in love with, Rashid had been furious. It was unthinkable that his younger brother should marry a foreigner. They had both seen what had happened in their own family. They knew mixed marriages didn't work.

An American! He had a mental image of a girl who chewed gum, talked loudly, wore too much makeup and gyrated to acid rock. He could barely hide his surprise when Jamal brought Katherine to meet him. She was a quiet young woman, shy and uncertain, obviously ill at ease. But she didn't chew gum and she wore almost no makeup. He had looked at her and suddenly the thought of Jamal making love to her had enraged him. He'd wanted to snatch her away from Jamal; instead he had snatched Jamal away from her.

Now he had possessed her. He had taken the woman who was betrothed to his brother. He had committed an unforgivable act. But it was an act for which he could not be sorry.

But what about Jamal? Jamal, whom he loved more as a father would love a son than the way one brother loved another. It had seemed to him when their father died that Jamal was his responsibility. He had loved the boy and tried to do what was best for him. Now he had taken a woman who belonged to Jamal. He had taken her and he knew that he would never let her go.

Sooner or later he would have to face Jamal and tell him. Rashid's arms tightened around Katherine. And he would have to ask him about the woman in Tangier.

For over a year now there had been rumors that Jamal was living with a woman in Tangier. He hadn't spoken to Jamal about this because his brother was of age; if he wanted to live with a woman that was his affair. But when Katherine came back into Jamal's life, Rashid had sent a man to Tangier. This was one of the reasons why he'd ordered Jamal to France; he wanted him out of the way while he checked.

But that wasn't the only reason, of course. He wanted Jamal out of Morocco while he tried to convince Katherine that Jamal wasn't the man for her—and that he was. But he'd made a mess of it. She hated him, hated him so much she'd risked her life to get away from him.

He rubbed his face against her hair. Katherine, he thought, Katherine. I'm obsessed with you. If I'd lost you to the desert I think I would have lost my mind. His arms tightened around her, but when she gave a small sound of protest he loosened his grasp and whispered, "Sleep, Katherine. Sleep, my love."

It had been almost three o'clock in the morning before he'd been able to get to the house after the storm. Fatima and the other servants had been waiting for him, their faces stricken with fear. Fatima had prostrated herself, weeping and wailing when he pulled her to her feet.

"The American woman is gone," Fatima cried. "She has disappeared into the *shergi,* the wind of the desert."

He wanted to go and look for her immediately, but even in his fear he knew he couldn't. Instead he organized his men, passing out canteens, rations and guns. He divided the men into separate search parties and at daybreak they rode out into the desert.

He and Saoud found the jeep stuck in the sand, one end almost hidden from view. He called out as they approached, and was sick with disappointment when he found that Katherine had abandoned the vehicle. He sent Saoud in one direction while he went the opposite way, trying not to admit to himself that there was little hope. He had known of this oasis, but the chances of Katherine's stumbling on it were a hundred to one. But something told him that was where he should go.

It had been hard going on horscback, even with an animal like Corsair. He'd ridden the horse hard. When at last he saw the oasis he'd slowed Corsair, and standing in the stirrups had looked frantically for a sign of life, crying aloud in despair when he saw no movement. Then suddenly he'd seen her at the edge of the pool, almost naked, her fair hair streaming down over her shoulders.

When finally she was in his arms, the joy and anger and passion had gotten all mixed up and he'd taken her, like some wild brute, there on the sand.

"Forgive me, my love," he whispered as he kissed

the top of her head. "I can't let you go now—now that I know what magic could be between us."

He had to get them out of here. Tomorrow, he told himself when he felt his eyelids droop. I'll think of something tomorrow. Have to sleep . . . tired . . . so tired.

So tired that he didn't hear the first faint rustle of wind in the palms or see the gathering clouds cover the stars. He moved closer to Katherine and his arms tightened protectively around her. The wind stirred her hair, brushing it across his face and chest. But neither of them woke.

It was Corsair who gave the first warning, neighing as he strained on the reins that held him. Suddenly Rashid woke and saw the warning signs, the hiss of palm fronds in the wind, the stir of dust.

He put his hand on Katherine's shoulder. "Wake up!" His voice was urgent. "There's a storm coming."

Rolling to his feet as she sat up and reached for her caftan, he grabbed his burnoose and pulled it over his head. "Pull the headpiece around so that it covers your nose. We're in for a *shergi*. Fill both the canteens with fresh water. Then gather as many dates as you can. There's fruit and bread in the saddlebag. I'm going to water Corsair. Then I'll try to fix some kind of a shelter for us."

He knew how bad this could be. Sometimes these *shergis* went on for days. The sands would drift, covering the date palms, even covering the water holes. This was a small oasis and vulnerable to a severe storm.

There was a three-foot wall of rock that someone had built at another time, probably against the same kind of storm they were in for now. As he set about trying to find rocks to add to it he saw that the sky had darkened in just a few minutes and that the wind had picked up. The sand swirled, making it difficult to see further than a few feet. When he glanced at Katherine he saw the caftan blowing around her legs and against her body. She stood near the water, looking out at the desert, hands clenched to her sides.

"Bring the food over here," he called, knowing that if he kept her busy she wouldn't have time to worry about the storm. "Gather up some rocks. We've got to build up this wall."

They worked for over an hour. Corsair grew more and more restive. Rashid let the horse drink again and then he tied him closer to the enclosure. By now the wind was so bad they could barely see and finally Rashid said, "All right, that's all we can do. You've got the canteens?"

When she nodded he reached for one and slung it around his neck. "Put the other one around yours," he said.

They sat with their backs against the wall as the day grew darker and the wind grew stronger. "Keep your head down," Rashid told her. "Try to cover your nose and your mouth."

Katherine's eyes were wide with fright. The storm the other night, the night she had escaped, had been bad. But not like this. She felt blinded by the sand, smothered in it. Everything focused on this one small spot in the desert, this hot howling wind, this man beside her.

So much had happened to her, both physically and emotionally, that she felt drained, depleted. She knew her survival depended on Rashid—they would live or perish together.

He had taken her by force yesterday. But later he had aroused her as no other man ever had. She was not a sexual innocent, but she hadn't even dreamed she could feel the way Rashid had made her feel. She hated him, yet she had responded to him. Now her life depended on him.

Hours passed and the wind grew worse. Corsair strained at the reins, neighing in fright. Rashid went to him time and time again, his head bent against the force of the storm as he tried to reassure the animal.

"When will it end?" Katherine shouted. "How long can this go on?"

"It could end by nightfall. But sometimes . . ." He hesitated.

"Sometimes what?"

"It's rare, but sometimes it can go on for several days."

"Several days? Can we survive that long?"

"Of course we can. Don't be foolish. We've got water and we've got food. It'll be fine—we've just got to wait it out, that's all. Why don't you try to sleep?"

Sleep! she thought. I can't even breathe. She put her head down on her knees, trying to blot out the sound of the wind, the sharp sting of sand against her body. She slept for a while but when she felt Rashid stir beside her she opened her eyes to see that the sand had drifted over the wall and that he was trying to scoop it out with his hands. Quickly she knelt beside him and, taking off her slippers, began to scoop sand with them. When she lifted her head she could see over the wall, see sand piled high against the date palms.

When they'd gotten out as much of the sand as they could Katherine said, "I'm thirsty. Should I drink from the canteen?"

Rashid shook his head. "It's better to drink from the pond while we can." He grasped her hand. "Come on, let's make a run for it."

The wind hit her with a terrible force, throwing her against Rashid. Together they struggled toward the water and when they reached it he motioned her to get down on her stomach to drink. With growing dismay Katherine saw that there was sand in the water. She brushed it away, then scooped the cool liquid up in her hands to drink. After she drank her fill she said, "What about Corsair?"

Rashid nodded and after he had quenched his thirst he went to the stallion. The great horse rolled his eyes in fright and reared back, almost jerking the reins from Rashid's hand.

"Easy," Rashid soothed. "Easy, boy." He relaxed his hold while Corsair drank, one hand on the horse's flank, the reins in his other hand.

Suddenly the wind grew stronger, bending the palms, sending a frond flying across Corsair's head. The horse reared up too swiftly for Rashid to tighten his hold on the reins.

"Corsair!" Rashid cried. But it was too late. With a frenzied whinny the stallion bolted.

"Catch him!" Katherine screamed as she ran to the edge of the oasis. "He'll die out there!" The wind tore at her, whipping her hair around her face. She looked as though she wanted to run out into the desert after the stallion.

"Get back behind the shelter," Rashid ordered.

"Corsair's gone. There's nothing we can do about it now."

"But he'll—" She stopped, white teeth biting hard on her lower lip.

"He'll die." His voice was harsh with pain. "He'll die out there and there isn't a damn thing I can do about it."

The wind raged all that night. A dozen times Katherine and Rashid scooped sand out of their fortlike shelter. When they weren't doing that they tried to rest, their backs against the stone wall. Rashid pulled her close to him, trying to shield her from the wind and the sand. All she could see of him were the dark eyes peering at her from the turban covering his head and his face. He was a desert man now, an Arab, a man from a different time.

The storm went on all the next day. The only time they moved from the shelter of the rocks was to drink from the pool that was by now half filled with sand. They ate the fruit and chewed the hard bread. The rest of the time they huddled together.

The wind stopped some time the next night and they slept. When they woke they looked about them. The shape of the desert had changed. Some of the date palms were almost covered by mounds of sand. The pond had disappeared.

"What will we do now?" Katherine asked when she came to stand beside Rashid.

"We move on," he said in an expressionless voice.

"Move on? But . . . but where?" The thought of going out into the desert again filled her with sickening fear.

"We can't stay here, Katherine. There isn't any more

water." He put his hands on her shoulders and turned her so that she faced him. "But we have the canteens and we have food. My men are out looking for us. Either they'll find us or we'll find another oasis. We're going to be all right."

She looked around the ruin of the oasis. Rashid was right, they couldn't stay here. But as she gazed out at the desert she felt her body tense with fear. She didn't want to go out there, out to the vast and unknown nothingness of the desert.

"Let's get going," he prodded.

She adjusted the canteen that hung around her neck. Then, with one last look at the oasis said, "I'm ready."

Chapter 11

THE FIRST FEW HOURS WERE NOT TOO BAD, BUT BY NOON the desert was an inferno. Silence brooded over the sun-scorched sand. Dunes, like the towers of a dream city, rose against the clear blue sky. Heat shimmered in an endless sea of light, hurting their eyes, blinding them as they peered out at the desert through dark enveloping folds of cloth.

"Eat a few dates," Rashid told her. "Keep a pit in your mouth, it will help."

Katherine tried not to complain. She'd never felt so dirty or so hot in her life. If only she could have had a bath in the pool before they left. She wondered if it would ever spring to life again, if it would ever save someone else as it had saved her.

Think of something, she ordered herself. Think of a crisp fall day in Maine, of the way the leaves turn and a nip of frost in the air. Remember the crash of the waves along the coast, the bite of saltwater against your skin. Remember the lobster bakes on the shore, the taste of cold beer on your tongue.

She closed her eyes, sucking hard on the date pit.

By late afternoon she knew she couldn't go much further. They drank a few sips of water and ate the last piece of fruit. When night fell they sank down on the sand and before they slept drank the last of the water from Katherine's canteen.

"We have the other one," Rashid said when he saw her look of fear. "It will last us another day."

And after that? Katherine wondered. What happens after that?

They spoke little that night. It was as though the sun had drained all of their energy, all of their emotion. They slept fitfully, and started walking again at dawn.

At midday Katherine began to think about dying. It suddenly seemed terribly important that she didn't die dirty. If Rashid would let her have her half of the water, she'd tell him she'd decided to wash with it instead of drinking it. He could rant and rave all he wanted, but it was her water and she'd do what she wanted with it.

"I refuse to die without a bath," she declared.

"Katherine?" He put his hand on her arm, stopping her. "Let's rest for a minute and have a drink of water."

"No thank you. I prefer to bathe in mine."

Dark brows came together in a frown. He opened the canteen and handed it to her. When she shook her head he said, "It's all right, Katherine. There'll be enough for a bath later."

"Are you sure?" she said suspiciously.

"Yes, I'm sure. But you really must drink a little now."

She took a sip, licking her parched and swollen lips. "That's enough," she said. "I want to save the rest."

He tore off a corner of his burnoose and wet it. Then he shoved the shawl back from her feverish face and said, "Why don't we rinse your face now? That'll make you feel better."

"And cleaner." She closed her eyes. "I feel better with that thing off my head. I don't want to wear it anymore."

"You have to." He put his arm around her waist and began to walk.

"I want to rest a while," she protested.

"Walk!" he commanded. "Walk!"

One foot ahead of the other. One step at a time. A giant step. May I take a giant step? Yes you may. Sand shifted under her feet, making her stagger. "Oops," she said. "Getting a little tired. Too much sun. Time to go in now."

"Keep going, Katherine," the man beside her said.

She began to hum to herself, then suddenly, abruptly, stopped and thought, I'm going to die. Well! Well, well, well!

That was when she saw the hooded black figures coming toward her over a sand dune. Come to carry her off . . . to the sweet by and by where we'll meet on that far distant shore. . . .

Then it didn't seem to her that she had to struggle

anymore, so with a sigh she let go and sank down into a blessed black nothingness.

Water dribbled down her chin. A hand raised her head and she opened her mouth and drank before she lapsed again into unconsciousness.

When next she woke, she was braced against Rashid and they were mounted on a horse. Although it seemed to be early evening, the air still hadn't cooled.

"So hot," she complained. Then with her head against his chest she drifted off again.

Later, when she woke, clad only in her bra and panties, a strange woman with a tattoo on her forehead was bathing her.

"Where's Rashid?" Katherine asked.

The woman looked at her without answering. Then she handed her a clean white robe and left. By the time Katherine had put the robe on the woman returned with a bowl of rice and meat.

Katherine sat up and when she saw there wasn't a fork, she dipped into the dish with her fingers. She took two bites and said again, "Where is Rashid? The man I was with?" She indicated somebody tall, with broad shoulders, and tried to frown like he did.

"Ah!" The woman put both hands under her head and made a snoring sound. Then she pointed to the food and to Katherine's mouth.

"Okay." Katherine dipped her fingers into the bowl. "But this may take some getting used to."

After she had eaten the woman brought her a glass of hot mint tea. She pointed to herself and shouted, "Zahira. Zahira."

Katherine nodded. "Katherine," she said as she took the glass and nodded her thanks.

For the first time she looked around. She was in a large black tent. All of the sides were rolled up. Rugs, like the one she had been lying on, partly covered the ground. There were pillows and a small low table off to one side. Other than that the tent was empty.

Two women stooped low to enter. They stared at her. No one spoke. Finally Zahira pointed to Katherine and indicated that she should sleep. Katherine nodded, and when the women left she lay back down on the rug.

It seemed that a miracle had happened: She and Rashid had been saved. She didn't know where she was or who these people were, but for now at least she was alive and she was safe.

It was daylight when she woke. Rashid was on his knees beside her and on the table was a pot of mint tea and two glasses.

"How do you feel this morning?"

"All right, I think. I slept well." She sat up and stretched. "Where are we?"

"In a nomad camp."

"How did we get here? I remember seeing some dark-robed men coming over a dune but I thought . . ." She stopped, embarrassed.

"You thought what, Katherine."

"That they were death coming to take me to the sweet by and by."

"The sweet by and by?"

"It's a hymn I knew when I was a child."

"I see." He clamped down hard on his lower lip and looked away for a moment before he said, "The nomads had been visiting another camp. They brought us here."

"Allah must have been watching over us," she said, trying to keep her voice light. "What will we do now?"

"I've talked to the head man. His name is Mustafa Madih. He doesn't have any camels now because some of his men have gone to Tafilet. It's a long trip, but as soon as they come back and have rested they'll take us to Erfoud."

"When will they be back?"

"Not for several weeks."

"Several weeks!" She stared at Rashid in disbelief. "You mean we have to stay here for . . . for weeks?"

"I'm afraid so."

"But isn't there any other way we can get out?"

"There are horses, but Mustafa says they can't make that long a trip. I'm sorry."

"Sorry?" She looked around with desperate eyes. "Everyone will think we're dead. My father and mother—" Her voice broke.

"I'm sorry," Rashid said again. "Believe me when I tell you I didn't mean to cause you such pain. I wish there was something I could do, but there isn't. We have to make the best of this."

"If you hadn't tricked me into flying with you . . . if you hadn't—"

"I know what I did was wrong," he broke in. "Once we leave this place I'll try to make everything right again. Meantime all we can do is wait. It's just a matter of a few weeks."

"A matter of weeks!"

"These are decent people, Katherine. No harm will come to us. Mustafa has given us this tent—"

"Given *us?* You mean we have to stay here together?"

"I told him you were my wife." He held up a cautioning hand. "It was the only way I could protect you. There are single men here. If they think you belong to me they won't bother you." His voice hardened. "So for the time that we're here you'll conduct yourself as though you were my wife, especially in front of the others. When I tell you to do something you'll do it. You won't talk back to me in front of these people. Is that clear?"

"I'll do as I please," she snapped.

"You do and you'll get a cuff on the side of the head, the same as these women do when they talk back to their men."

Katherine shot him a hate-filled look and he said, "I have to behave like one of them while we're here. I have no choice and neither do you."

He handed her the makeup case. "Here," he said, "maybe this will improve your disposition." Then before she could answer he left the tent.

Katherine glared at his retreating back, wanting to sling the case at him. Instead she opened it and reached for the mirror. She was a mess! Her face was burned, her lips swollen. And her hair! She could have wept. Instead she got up and went out of the tent to look around.

It was a city of large black tents in the middle of nowhere. There were a few tall scraggly palms, smaller date palms, patches of green and several pools of water. Goats and sheep grazed, trying to find small shrubs between the rocks, and several horses were tied under a canopy.

The minute Katherine stepped two feet away from the tent she was surrounded by silent children, who looked at her with large dark eyes.

"Hi." Katherine smiled. "I'm looking for some water." She cupped her hand, pretending to drink.

"Al má," a boy of about ten said.

"Al má," Katherine repeated.

A woman, dressed in a light-colored robe, came out of one of the tents. She was not veiled, but her hands and feet were tinted with henna.

"Al má," Katherine said, and pointed to her hair.

"Ah." The woman nodded and said something to the boy. He disappeared and a few moments later returned lugging two pails of water.

"Shûkrán," Katherine said. "Thank you." With the children tagging behind she went to the entrance of her tent and, kneeling down, doused her hair in one of the pails of water and began to scrub it with the bar of scented soap she had brought from Rashid's.

The children stared at her fair hair in fascination. She held the soap out so a little girl, braver than the rest, could smell it. The child wrinkled her nose and giggled. Katherine dunked her head into the bucket again and all the children laughed. Then the boy who had brought her the water tapped her on the shoulder. He motioned her to bend down so that he—very strong, he indicated, showing her the muscles in his upper arms—could pour the other pail of water over her head.

Katherine nodded, yipping in dismay when the boy, instead of pouring it little by little, dumped all of it in one huge splash.

He looked as shocked as Katherine did when she raised her head, gasping. But then she grinned and tousled his hair, while the children around them burst into ripples of laughter.

The boy pointed to himself. "Abdur," he said. He was barefoot and wore ragged dusty pants. His nose was straight, his mouth gently curved. But it was the sweetness of expression in his wide black eyes that held Katherine's attention. He was one of the handsomest children she'd ever.seen, she thought as she smiled at him. Then pointing to herself she said, "Katherine."

Arched black brows came together in a frown. "Kat-ar-een?"

"Yes."

"Yes," Abdur repeated. Then he grabbed the buckets and ran to get her more water.

Rashid, just coming out of one of the tents, stopped to watch her with the children. A slow smile curved his mouth.

When the evening shadows lengthened to dusk, he came to the tent they were to share.

"Zahira is cooking our dinner tonight," he said. "Tomorrow she'll show you how to prepare the food so that from now on you'll cook for us."

"I have no intention of cooking for you," Katherine snapped.

"You will if you want to eat." Rashid got up and took two bowls from Zahira when she appeared. *"Shûkrán,"* he said. He came back, sat cross-legged on the rug and handed one of the bowls to Katherine.

They ate without speaking and when they were finished and the dishes had been rinsed and put aside, Katherine glanced at him. Her eyes were wary. She had already picked a spot at the far end of the tent where she intended to sleep. Just as she was about to move toward it Rashid said, "Just a moment. I want to talk to you."

He got up and began to lower the tent flaps. When he came back he said, "I've thought about our relationship and there are some things we have to talk about. Would you like to sit down?"

"I prefer to stand."

"Very well." His gaze met hers as he continued. "When I took you from Rabat it was with the idea of talking you out of a marriage to Jamal and trying to talk you into a relationship with me. That was a suggestion you seemed to find . . . reprehensible."

"You're right so far."

"You would have lived well, Katherine. We'd have divided our time between the desert, my home in Casablanca and the apartment in Paris. I wanted to dress you in silk and bedeck you with jewels. You could have had your hair done in the finest Parisian salons." A wry smile tugged at his lips. "But instead an Arab boy pours a bucket of well water over your head because I've brought you to this."

Before she could step back he reached for her and put his hands on her shoulders so she couldn't pull away. In a quiet voice he said, "Look at me, Katherine."

In the evening shadows his face was ruggedly handsome. The clean white robe only seemed to emphasize his masculinity, the width of his shoulders, the broadness of his chest. He moved closer. She could smell the scent of the desert on his skin and see the passion of the desert in his eyes.

His expression was solemn, his voice quiet when he

said, "I'm sorry, Katherine. This wasn't what I had planned for you. But there isn't anything I can do about it now. When we get back to civilization I'll let you go—if you still want to—but for whatever time we have here in the desert we're going to be together."

Katherine's eyes widened in question. "Together?" she said slowly.

"In every sense of the word."

When she backed away from him he reached out to stop her. "For the weeks that we're here you'll be my mistress, my wife, my love. I'm going to have my way, Katherine, with or without your consent." He took her hand, brought it to his lips and continued more softly, "I suspect you feel things for me you're afraid to admit, even to yourself. This is my chance to show you how it could be for us. If I can't convince you that there's something very special between us, then I'll let you go."

"There's nothing between us." Katherine jerked her hand away. "There'll never be anything." Turning her back she started out of the tent, but before she could take two steps Rashid scooped her up in his arms.

"I'm going to do my damnedest to prove you're wrong," he said. The strong arms tightened around her. She felt the brush of his lips against her cheek. Before she could protest, he carried her to a pile of rugs and pillows at one end of the tent and, when she struggled against him, he dropped her on them. Kneeling over her, he said, "I want it to be like it was at the oasis when I found you. I want you to cry my name again. I want you to lift your body to mine the way you did before."

His eyes, hooded with desire, burned into hers. He

looked like a desert chieftan, a warrior out of the Arabian nights.

She felt the thudding beat of her heart, the flame of remembrance whisper through her trembling body.

"No," she protested. "It wasn't like that."

"You're a beautiful liar." He pushed her back against the rugs and his mouth found hers. "Liar," he said again as his tongue, like a hot dagger, stabbed past her lips to invade the recesses of her mouth. His body was over hers, holding her pinned to the ground while he kissed her.

Katherine fought him, her fingers tightening in his thick black hair to try to force him away from her. But his mouth continued to devour her and his hands moved over her body.

Suddenly he sat up and yanked his robe off, then, pulling her to a sitting position, drew the white garment over her head. When he saw the wisps of lace that partially covered her, he bent to kiss the fullness spilling over the delicate bra. She struck out at him and he grabbed her wrists in one hand, holding them while he buried his face between her breasts.

"You smell so good," he whispered as he slipped the bra off her shoulders. His arms went around her, holding her close while his lips moved to her temple, then down the line of her jaw to kiss the tender skin behind her ear. Holding her so that she was helpless against him, he kissed her breasts.

"I love these," he whispered against the fullness. "Some day when I'm not as hungry for you as I am now I'm going to kiss them for hours. I'm going to kiss them until you beg me to stop."

His tongue, a dart of fire, touched one peaked nipple

and when she quivered, jumping as though she'd been burned, he lapped at it, teasing with his tongue until she cried aloud. Then his mouth found hers and he kissed her, taking her lower lip between his teeth while his tongue caressed it.

Katherine dug her nails into his skin and when he flinched she managed to pull away from him. "Stop this," she pleaded. "Please stop. I hate it when you touch me. I—"

He covered the words with his mouth. His arms tightened around her and he turned her on her side, resting his head on her arm so that she couldn't move, and captured her other hand. Again his mouth went to her breasts and his tongue scorched circles of fire around and around her nipples, kissing them, thrilling with excitement when she trembled against him.

She was held, captured by his body and the hands that touched her, the lips that burned against her skin. In the fading light of the tent she could see that his eyes were closed. His long lashes made quarter-moon shadows against his cheek. For a moment she closed her eyes and allowed herself to surrender to the warmth that flooded her body. Not even aware that she was doing it, she moved closer into the circle of his arms with a small purr of pleasure.

His lips were infinitely gentle now as they left her breasts to travel down her body, feathering kisses that left her breathless with desire. He kissed the inside of her thighs and she gasped. "Don't," she whispered as his lips traveled upward. "No one has ever—"

"Then I'll be the first. I'll be the only and the last." He grasped her hands and, bringing them to her sides, held her while she writhed against him. Her body was on fire; her nerve ends, like tiny electric wires, shot bolt after bolt of live current through her. She heard, as though from a distance, her own frantic whimperings.

When he let go of her hands to reach for her breasts, she grasped his shoulders, meaning to thrust him away from her, but instead she caressed with the hands that had meant to wound.

When her breath came in gasps of pleasure and she began to tremble, he let her go and with a hoarse cry came up over her and joined his body to hers. Holding her shoulders, he pulled her closer as he moved deep within her, carrying her up and up on a tide of feeling that was beyond joy, beyond ecstasy.

"Katherine," he cried against her lips as his body, strong now with need, moved against her. His hips ground against hers as she lifted herself to meet his every thrust and heard his sighs of pleasure.

She was reaching now, reaching for that ultimate rainbow of feeling, quivering with need as she smothered her cry against his shoulder, whispering his name as she felt his arms tighten around her, as he buried his face against her hair and shuddered over her in an agony of pleasure.

Afterward Katherine tried to move away, but he held her close in his embrace.

"Let me go," she whispered, her hands against his chest.

"Shhh," he said. "Shhh," and began to caress the length of her with gentle hands until finally she sighed against him and went to sleep.

Chapter 12

ZAHIRA WAS A WOMAN OF INDETERMINATE AGE. HER BODY seemed to be all awkward bends, angles and bones with barely enough flesh to cover them. Her features were sharp. She had a nose like an angry hawk, small piercing eyes and ears that stood at attention. She wore a tattered green sweatshirt under her white robe and bound her lank hair with a piece of white cloth. Silver coins, bangles and beads jangled around her thin neck. When she talked she waved her arms, hissing with impatience because Katherine couldn't understand her.

She was a good teacher but a hard taskmaster. Under the best of conditions Katherine was not the world's greatest cook, but with a charcoal brazier in the middle of the Sahara she was a disaster. She burned the goat meat, ruined the shishkabob and dropped the wheat cakes onto the burning coals.

Rashid did not complain about the meals she set before him. There were times when his lips quirked in amusement and once or twice a look of absolute horror crossed his face when he tasted a piece of meat. But he never voiced his dismay and little by little Katherine's cooking improved. Finally the day came when her shishkabob was cooked to perfection and her wheat cakes were actually tasty.

"An excellent meal," Rashid said as he ate the dessert of figs and dates. "You're getting to be quite a cook."

"I have no choice, as you said. Especially with that hag Zahira hovering over me like a great bony vulture."

"Zahira's all right," Rashid said with a laugh. "She likes you. She told me that if I beat you with a stick now and then I might even make a good Arab woman out of you."

Katherine glared at him. She'd been glaring at him for the past few days. She cooked his meals and washed his clothes, but she offered no pleasantries. He'd taken her away from her own world and brought her to this godforsaken desert against her will. His lovemaking was fiercely passionate. The more Katherine resisted, the more determined he was to make her respond. She fought against him and against herself, but there were times when it was impossible to stay aloof from the urgencies he awakened in her body.

Each morning, as the first faint light of dawn streaked the desert sky, while still she slept she would feel the soft caress of a hand on her breasts. Reluctant to wake, trying to slide back into a dream, she would mumble a sleepy complaint, then feel a finger under her chin and the soft pressure of his mouth on hers. Half awake and half asleep, she would feel the warmth of passion grow and spread. Then, with a sigh, she would feel his body ease over hers.

It was on these slumberously sensual mornings that, in spite of all Rashid had done to her, she would feel a stirring deeper than passion. If he had uttered one word of tenderness then, one word of love, she might have turned to him and gladly given all she had.

But he had no words of love to give her, only the demands of his body. And Katherine hated him for that.

"What is it?" he said now, breaking in on her thoughts.

"Nothing. It's nothing." She refused to meet his gaze. "Well, it's . . . Zahira. She wanted to put henna on my hands and feet today. She said it would make me beautiful and that it would keep the *jinn* away. What's *jinn?*"

"The evil spirits. They're not supposed to like the scent of henna." He chuckled. "The next thing you know she'll want to tattoo you." His voice changed. "If you ever do wear a tattoo, Miss Katherine, you know where it will be."

She glanced at him, feeling hot color creep to her cheeks, remembering the night he had marked her with his teeth.

He took her hand in his. "I don't want any henna on these hands," he said in a lighter tone. "They're lovely just as they are."

"I thought you wanted me to be a good Arab woman."

"I wanted you to understand what being an Arab

wife meant. I wanted you to be aware of what you were in for if you married Jamal."

"It's not the same for mistresses?" Her yellow eyes narrowed with anger.

"No, as a matter of fact, it isn't. A mistress is different."

"Different? Oh, you mean a mistress is a luxury, like an expensive car—an *imported* car in my case. That's why you'd dress me in European clothes, I suppose."

"Damn it, Katherine, that's not it at all." He pushed away from the table and she knew he was angry.

"Besides," she went on, "you can leave a mistress because you have no moral or legal responsibility. When you're tired of her you pat her on the head, toss her a bauble or two and walk away. No tears, no ties, no commitments. No bond of love or law to hold you."

Furious now, she glared at him. "Did you honestly think I'd fall into your arms when you asked me to be your mistress, Rashid? Did you think for even a minute I'd let you buy me?"

"It's not like that!" His face was white with anger. Without another word he turned away and strode out of the tent into the darkness of the night.

For a reason Katherine couldn't define her eyes filled with tears. Damn him, damn her, damn everything! She was behaving like a witch. A wife! When he made love to her she all but swooned with pleasure. She hated herself for the small cries she couldn't hold back, hated the way her body responded to his and hated him for making her respond. Each time she did she vowed she never would again. But oh sweet heaven, the touch of his lips on hers, the feel of his body against hers in the night made her forget everything.

Finally she went to sit in the opening of the tent and after a while she felt her anger fade. This was the time she liked best of these days in the desert, this quiet time just before darkness when the setting sun cast shadows of red and bronze and gold upon the shifting sands and the sky turned a myriad of unbelievable radiant hues. Piping voices of children came from the tents, then little by little faded until a hush settled over the night.

They'd been here a little over a week but she no longer felt strange. It seemed to her now as she gazed out across the distant sands that she'd always been a part of this desert world and that a part of her would weep when she had to leave. She'd miss little Abdur, who had become her friend, and yes, she'd even miss Zahira.

And Rashid? she asked herself. Will you miss him? Will you miss his frown, the way he looks at you with his warm desert eyes? Will you miss his caresses, the touch of his lips against your skin?

When at last she went into the tent she lowered the flaps, bathed from one of the pails of water Rashid brought every day and changed into the short gauzelike gown she had brought with her.

She was asleep when Rashid came in, but she woke sometime in the night and felt him beside her. He stirred in his sleep and took her hand. For a long time he didn't move, then with a low groan he pulled her to him.

His hands were warm against the thin material of her gown. He didn't try to take it off her, but touched her through it, caressing her wordlessly while she tried to lie stiff and unfeeling.

Don't respond, she told herself. Don't! She clamped

her lower lip, dug her nails into her palms and willed her body to be still. When he began to kiss her breasts—taking through the gauze the already erect peaks with his teeth—she put her fist to her mouth to keep from crying out. And when he raised the gown over her hips she tried to move away from him.

But he held her, covering her with the length of his body. His mouth sought hers, and when she didn't respond he moved to kiss her breasts again.

I won't respond, Katherine told herself. I'll lie here and I won't move, I won't touch him, I won't whisper his name. Arms straight down to her sides, fists clenched, she closed her eyes while he kissed the fullness of her breasts. But she didn't move, didn't flinch and finally with a cry of frustration Rashid grasped her hips and joined his body to hers.

"Damn you," he cried as he plunged against her. "Let go! Let yourself do what you want to do." He pressed his hard body against hers, demanding a response she refused to give, though her body was afire with longing.

"Damn you," he said against her clenched teeth, and suddenly it was over. His body shuddered against hers as his hands fastened in her hair and his legs tightened around her hips. Finally, with a gasp, he pulled away from her.

For a long moment he didn't speak and then, in a voice trembling with anger, said, "I swear before Allah that I'll never touch you again. Never!"

But in his heart he knew that he lied. That tomorrow, and for all the tomorrows they had left, he would make love to her. He couldn't help himself—for he had done something he'd sworn he would not do. He had fallen in love with her.

A few days later the camp was a hubbub of talk. The Arabian horses were brushed and groomed. All of the men between seventeen and seventy were in a fever of excitement.

"What's all the commotion about?" Katherine asked Rashid.

"There's going to be a *Fantasia.*" Seeing her bewildered look he added, "It's an exhibition of horsemanship. There's a holiday coming up and there'll be festivities—something like a county fair in your country, I imagine. There'll be dancing, games for the children and then the *Fantasia.* That's all I'm going to tell you. You'll see for yourself soon enough."

Three days later nomads began coming in from other oases, and for the first time since she'd been in the camp Katherine heard the sound of music, flutes and tambourines, that sounded like a symphony to her music-starved ears.

"*Aegee!* Come," Zahira cried, fastening her bony hand around Katherine's wrist, leading her to where a group of women sat in a circle chattering among themselves. In another circle sat the men, dressed in white djellabas, silver daggers hanging at their waists. Most of them played a strange funnel-shaped drum. Little by little the rhythm and beat of the drums increased. The circle of women began to sway to the tempo.

Suddenly the women jumped to their feet and threw off their dark shawls to reveal their bright-colored dresses and necklaces of silver coins. They began to dance, slowly and solemnly, moving together to the right, then back and to the left, their necklaces jingling to the rhythm of the drums, their bright skirts swirling around their bare ankles as they raised their arms, chanting in time to the music.

Abruptly the music stopped. The women stood still, waiting.

"Fantasia!" a voice cried. *"Fantasia, fantasia."*

Everyone began to run toward an open space at the edge of the oasis. Katherine, with Zahira still gripping her arm, ran with them.

It was a scene right out of the Arabian Nights, Katherine thought. Dozens of men, all wearing white djellabas and turbans, long Berber rifles held aloft, paraded past the women on splendid Arabian horses. When they passed she saw Rashid. He sat tall in the saddle, his face bronzed by the sun, proud chin thrust forward.

She felt the quickening of her heart, the beat of pulse in her throat, a kindling of warmth in her body. When he turned and saw her she tried to look away, but could not. For a long moment they gazed at each other, then the line of horsemen moved on.

After the parade the riders wheeled their mounts and rode out toward the desert sands. Finally they stopped and turned back, forming a straight line. Then one of the men raised his rifle, shouted a resounding cry and the horses leapt forward.

Faster and faster they came, rifles raised, shouting, "O Allah! O Mohammed!"

Suddenly they let go of their reins and threw their rifles into the air. Then, catching the weapons in midair, they fired. The shots rang out as one explosive single sound.

In a cloud of dust the riders wheeled and raced back toward the desert, shouting their war cries and shooting their rifles in the air. When they pulled on the reins the horses neighed with excitement and galloped at breakneck speed back to the crowd, the men standing in the stirrups, arms raised, rifles aloft. They were brigands, warriors from another age, crying their battle cry as they charged. Wild and untamed they came, reckless and brave. But suddenly a cry went up as two riders crashed together. One of them flew off his horse and thudded to the ground. The other went down with his mount.

Instantly the other riders pulled up, jumped off their horses and ran to the fallen men. Before they could reach him, the first man attempted to get up, but fell back. But the other man lay still, his horse half covering him. As the horse struggled to his feet one of the riders knelt beside the man. There was a murmured discussion, then two of the men picked the fallen rider up.

The women pressed closer, and Katherine, caught in the crush, moved with them. She couldn't see the unconscious man at first, then suddenly caught a glimpse of his face. "Rashid!" she cried. "Rashid!"

She started forward, and when Zahira tried to hold her back she struck out at the woman, knocking her aside as she rushed to Rashid.

"Take him to the tent," she cried, then realizing they didn't understand her, she pointed to the black tent she and Rashid shared.

When they laid him down on the rugs she said, "Water, *al má. Al má.*"

One of the men brought her a pail and another, the head man Mustafa Madih, slipped the turban off Rashid's head. Katherine saw a knot the size of a golfball on his forehead. When she pressed a wet cloth against it, Rashid groaned.

"Don't move," Katherine said. "Lie still."

She felt his arms. One wrist was swollen but she didn't think it was broken. Mustafa watched her for a moment, then began to examine Rashid's legs. When he raised the djellaba Katherine saw that one leg was scraped and bloody. But when she gasped in concern Mustafa shook his head, trying to indicate, she supposed, that the injury wasn't serious. He flexed the leg to show her it wasn't broken.

"Okay," he said. "Okay."

Okay? Rashid looked terrible! His face was so still, so pale. She wet the cloth again and held it against the knot on his head. "Rashid? Rashid?"

His eyelids fluttered.

"Wake up, Rashid. Please wake up."

He opened his eyes and stared up at her. "What happened?"

"You fell."

Dark brows drew together in the familiar frown. "I've never fallen off a horse in my life!" He saw the men crowded around him and said something in Arabic. The men answered, gesturing as they talked, nodding at his questions. Several of them tried to speak at the same time. Then finally Mustafa patted Rashid's shoulder and motioned for the others to let him rest.

When they were alone Rashid said, "The other man has a broken arm and a crushed ankle." He started to get up, supporting himself on his sprained wrist, but with a low whistle of pain fell back on the rug. *"Zfft!"* he exclaimed, "is it broken?"

"No, I don't think so. But it's a bad sprain." She touched the lump on the side of his head. "How does your head feel?"

"Like it's been kicked by a very large horse." He tried again to sit up, but Katherine pushed him back down on the rug.

"Lie still," she ordered.

"I'm all right except for a headache."

"Rashid, lie still!" She got up and lowered the flaps of the tent. "You're going to rest now. I don't suppose there's even an aspirin here in the camp." She knelt beside him, wet the cloth again and placed it across his forehead and eyes. "I'll be right here if you want anything. I don't want you to move. Now rest." She put her hand on his shoulder and pushed him down.

He slept until early evening. The knot on his head seemed smaller but the area around it had turned an ugly green. He hardly spoke and when she asked him if his head still hurt he only nodded. He sipped a little of the mint tea she had prepared and allowed her to bathe him in cool water, submitting so docilely to her ministrations that it worried her.

In the morning his eyes were black and blue and the bruise on his head looked fierce and ugly. But the bump had gone down and his headache was better. Katherine helped him sit up to drink his tea and eat the wheat cakes she had prepared.

"You look worse than I do," he commented. "Didn't you sleep last night?"

"I slept enough." But she had barely closed her eyes, leaning over him every few minutes to make sure he was all right, terrified that something might happen to him.

He rested most of the day and by evening the headache had almost disappeared, so he went to see how the other injured man was faring. Katherine was sitting outside the tent with little Abdur when Rashid returned. He ruffled the boy's hair and said something to him. Abdur grinned. Rashid sat down cross-legged on the ground beside him and he and the boy talked until Abdur's mother came to call him.

"Good night." Abdur bowed to Katherine.

"Good night, Abdur. I'll see you tomorrow." When he disappeared into his own tent she said, "He's a nice boy. I'm going to miss him when we leave."

"That surprises me. I didn't think you'd miss anything about this place. I thought you hated it here almost as much as you hate me."

Katherine's face tightened.

"I haven't thanked you for taking care of me. It was kind of you to be concerned."

"I'd have been as concerned about anybody who'd been hurt." Then, realizing how harsh her words had sounded and wanting to make amends, she smiled slightly and said, "You look like a pirate."

"What?"

"A desert pirate. Your hair is too long and you need a shave. Your eyes are black and blue. With that white robe and your dark skin you look . . ." Her eyes lingered on his face. "You look . . ." But she couldn't go on because she was caught in the snare of his dark desert eyes. When he reached out and took her hand she didn't try to pull away from him.

"Do you really hate me so much, Katherine?" he

asked in a low voice. And when she didn't answer he got up and, pulling her to her feet, led her inside. There in the shadows he kissed her, his mouth warm against hers. "I want to make love to you," he whispered. "I want to hold you. I want to feel you naked in my arms."

"No." She stiffened, pulling away from him. But when she saw the sudden unexpected hurt in his eyes something seemed to move inside her and she continued, "You've been hurt, Rashid. You have to be careful."

"I'll be careful." He took her hand again, led her to where they slept and drew her down beside him. Kneeling, he faced her, pressing his body close to hers, his arms around her, one hand pressed to the small of her back so that he could feel the heat of her body against his.

My love, my love, he wanted to say, but did not.

Instead he laid her beside him on the rugs and his mouth found hers again.

Katherine could feel his urgency, feel it in the tenseness of his muscles, the thump of his heart and the quickening of his breath. She warmed to the touch of his lips, the long hard line of his body so close to hers.

She'd been so frightened the last two days. If something had happened to Rashid . . . The thought made her hands tighten against his back. If he'd been killed . . .

With a small cry Katherine moved closer to him, answering his kiss at last, parting her lips to welcome the warmth of his tongue, touching the tip of it with her own and feeling him shiver with pleasure.

His hands, stroking her through her robe, were warm and impatient. Without his asking she pulled it over her head and turned to help him do the same. At last they were naked, their bodies warm and close.

Perhaps it was the fear she'd known when he lay unconscious; perhaps it was the pent-up tension of the nights she'd refused to let her body yield to its demands —but now Katherine was unable to control her emotions. When Rashid cupped her breasts in his strong dark hands she gasped with pleasure.

He lay on his side and, pulling her into the curve of his arms, began to gently suckle one breast while his fingers caressed the other. Almost without thinking, Katherine began to stroke his strong bronze body. She curled her fingers in the black mat of chest hair, then roamed over his shoulders and down his arms, marveling in the feel, the texture of his skin. Finally, because she could not help herself, one hand moved downward. It was something she had never done and he groaned and whispered her name against her skin. With a low cry, Rashid rolled her onto her back, but when he raised himself over her he gave a sharp hiss of pain.

"What is it?" Katherine whispered, her eyes wide with concern.

"My wrist. It's all right, just give me a minute."

"No." Her voice was decisive. She took hold of his shoulders and forced him back on the rugs. Then she kissed him, her fair hair brushing his bare chest.

He looked up at her, his dark eyes widening in disbelief as she rested her body over his. "I just want to feel you like this for a moment," she murmured against his throat. "Feel the warmth of you under my body, the brush of your skin against mine."

"Katherine?" His arms tightened around her.

"Don't talk, Rashid. Don't say anything." She eased

herself onto his flanks. "Am I hurting your leg?" she whispered.

"No! God, no!" His voice was ragged as she lowered herself onto him.

Slowly she began to move. In the pale evening light she could see his face, see the eyes that had narrowed with desire, the strong flared nostrils, the glint of his white teeth. When he reached for her breasts she quickened her pace, giving small cries of delight as she moved against him, thrusting her breasts forward so that he could pleasure them.

"Katherine, Katherine." He said her name over and over again. "Katherine . . ."

When it was almost too much, she made herself go slower. Rashid's hands left her breasts to grasp her hips. "Don't stop," he cried.

"You make me wait," she whispered. "Now you have to."

Her body moved with agonizing slowness against his while he groaned with need. His fingers found her breasts again as she began to press against him. Then, suddenly, she was no longer in control. She was a wild thing, frantic with desire for this man. Her head was thrown back, her golden hair streamed down her back, her slim neck strained with effort as her hands tightened on his shoulders.

With one last surge of motion, as his hands gripped her waist and he cried her name, she spiraled up into a violent vastness of passion that was so intense it was almost unbearable.

Afterward she collapsed over him, trembling in the aftermath of love, her head buried in the hollow of his shoulder, quivering with pleasure as he caressed her.

She felt the touch of his lips against her temple and turned her face to find his mouth.

Oh, Rashid, she wanted to say. I don't know how this happened. I don't understand it. I only know I've never felt this way before, that I'll never feel this way again.

Finally, troubled and uncertain, she went to sleep with her body still covering his.

Chapter 13

THE CARAVAN OF CAMELS ARRIVED AT THE CAMP THREE days later. After they had rested for several days, Mustafa Madih chose two of the drivers to take Katherine and Rashid to Erfoud.

Their time in the desert had come to an end. All that would remain was the memory of black tents, of an endless expanse of golden sands and glorious sunsets. And of a man, Katherine thought. A man whose kisses I'll never forget.

She and Rashid were easier with each other now. It was as though they both knew their time together had almost ended. There had been so much anger, so much pain and passion. So many things said and unsaid.

On the day before she left, Abdur came to tell Katherine goodbye. She took her wristwatch off and placed it in his hand. It was a plain gold watch her father had given her when she graduated from college.

It had a second hand and it showed the date and the day of the week. Abdur had been fascinated by it and Katherine had let him wind it once or twice.

Now he held it in his hand, staring at it with unbelieving eyes as she tightened his hand around it. "From me to you," she said. "So that you'll remember the American lady."

His chin wobbled, he bobbed his head and said, *"Shûkrán."* Then he scrambled to his feet and ran toward his tent.

That night for dinner Katherine cooked shishkabob and the flat beans that Zahira, with much hissing and scolding, had taught her to prepare.

"This is pretty good," Rashid said with a smile. "Another few weeks out here and Zahira might make you a gourmet cook."

"Or hiss herself to death trying." Katherine refilled his bowl. "It's strange how you can adjust, isn't it?"

"Adjust?" The dark brows raised in question.

Katherine nodded. "I've grown accustomed to men wearing robes and women with tattooed faces and henna'd hands. When I get back to civilization it will be strange to see men in trousers and women with make-up." She made a face. "I doubt if I'll be able to cook as well in a microwave oven as I do over a brazier."

"Maybe you should take Zahira home with you."

"Allah forbid!" she said with a grin. Then suddenly she sobered. Home. Where was her home now? Where did she go from here? When Rashid had brought her to his home at the edge of the Sahara she'd been unable to understand his fascination for the desert. To her it had been a wasteland of heat and wind and shifting sands. But that had changed; she had changed. There was a rhythm, a mysticism about the desert that she now found strangely moving. She loved the special magic about this time of evening when the noises of the day were muted and campfires glowed in the gathering dusk, when there were still remnants of the setting sun and the sky was aglow with a miracle of color.

Tonight as she sat next to this man she had professed to hate and watched the rise of a full moon against the desert sky, Katherine felt a sadness almost too profound to bear. Perhaps Rashid sensed it, for when darkness settled over the camp he took her hand and said, "Come, let's walk for a while."

Silently they made their way through the camp, past the date palm trees, the tamarisk and the fig trees, to the edge of the sand dunes. When Katherine hesitated Rashid said, "We'll only go a little ways." Over the sweeping dunes into a world of quiet and solitude, following the path of the moon and the shadows of the sand.

When Katherine stopped, Rashid's arms encircled her waist and they stood for long minutes, her back against him, looking out into the desert night. When he let her go he pulled the burnoose over his head and spread it on the sand.

In the light of the moon his naked body was the most gracefully beautiful thing Katherine had ever seen. He stood, legs apart, looking down at her, smooth skinned, firm muscled, a bronze David.

They lay together on the burnoose, their bodies melding as one on the soft warm bed of desert sand. They kissed slowly and sweetly, both of them aware that this was the last time they would join in this act of love. For now, each of them secretly could call it love.

Her breasts were touched by moonlight when he bent to kiss them, her wheat hair turned to gold as it splayed over her bare shoulders.

Rashid whispered Arabic words she couldn't understand as he stroked her. At last he raised his body over hers and, looking deeply into her eyes, leaned to kiss her lips as he entered her. He moved slowly, languorously, savoring every moment. When Katherine lifted herself to him he found her mouth again, gently demanding.

Her hands traced tender patterns against his back, creeping down to touch the line of his firm round buttocks, loving the silky feel of them, the curves, the fullness.

Their rhythm was as quiet as the rhythm of the desert, the shifting, the sighing, the sudden swift cry when the passion deepened. The whispered pleas, the sweet urgings, the anxious questioning. The final "Yes, oh yes, oh yes . . ."

They lay together for a long time looking up at the million stars that were their ceiling, at the moon that was their light. But they didn't speak of all the things they were feeling, and when the desert air grew cool they put on their clothes and went back to the camp.

The small caravan that would take them back to Erfoud waited. The people of the camp crowded around to say their farewells. The women shook hands with Katherine, the men embraced Rashid and kissed him on both cheeks. The children gathered around—all of the children except Abdur.

When Katherine tried to ask the boy's mother where

he was the woman shook her head and said something to Rashid.

"He's in his tent," Rashid said. "His mother says he doesn't want to say goodbye to you again because he's afraid he'll cry in front of the other children."

"Would it be all right if I went into the tent?"

"His mother has suggested it."

Abdur was sitting cross-legged on the ground, his back to the entrance.

"I've come to say goodbye," Katherine said, kneeling beside him. She put her hand out. "Goodbye, Abdur. I'll never forget you."

The small Adam's apple worked. Finally he put his hand out. "Goodbye, Kat-er-een."

"I don't suppose I could give you a hug," she said. Then muttered, "Oh what the hell," and drew the boy into her arms. Before he could speak, she scrambled to her feet and hurried out of the tent.

"Ready?" Rashid asked, pretending not to notice her tears.

Katherine nodded. She turned again to say goodbye to the women and when she did Zahira pushed forward. She grabbed Katherine's hand and pumped it hard. Then she took a string of bright blue beads off, put them over Katherine's head and, turning on her heel, disappeared into the crowd of women.

Her chin trembling, Katherine looked at Rashid. "Let's go," she said. "Let's go before I change my mind and decide to stay in this godforsaken place."

The camel they had assigned her was an ugly, irascible creature that held its chin, with its drooping lip, up in the air as he looked down his nose at

Katherine. The driver yelled and whacked the creature across his legs. The camel knelt and Rashid helped her on. "Try to keep your legs back," he warned. "Camels are known for biting their riders."

"Wonderful!" She clutched the reins, hanging on for dear life as the beast lunged to his feet. "How long a trip is this going to be?"

"Four days. Don't worry, by tomorrow you'll be used to the sway. Just hang on. Keep your head and as much of your face covered as you can."

There were four of them in the caravan—Katherine and Rashid and the two drivers. Two extra camels were loaded with supplies.

When they waved to the villagers they turned the camels away from the camp and headed for the desert. Katherine couldn't help feeling a sudden moment of panic. She liked the desert when she had the protection of the camp, but twice it had almost killed her and she didn't relish the idea of going back into it.

They stopped at noon to eat a light lunch. Hanging onto the camel when he knelt was more scary than when he arose and Katherine cried out in alarm. But Rashid was there to catch her when she slid forward.

"You're doing fine," he said. "You'll have the hang of this in no time. How do you feel?"

"Like I'm still rocking. It isn't anything like a horse, is it?"

"No." His voice was quiet. "No, it isn't."

And Katherine knew he was thinking of Corsair.

By midafternoon Katherine was miserable. The heat and the constant swaying motion of the camel had made her queasy. She didn't say anything, but just hung onto the reins and tried to keep her feet out of the way of the spiteful beast. When they stopped at a small oasis Rashid helped her off. She would have fallen if he hadn't held her.

"What is it? Are you ill?"

"Seasick. If you laugh I'll kill you."

"I won't laugh. I've seen it happen to too many men." He led her to a shady place under the trees. "Sit here and I'll bring you some water."

She sipped the water and when one of the drivers handed her a rolled-up rug she spread it under a palm tree and went to sleep. She felt better when she woke and was able to eat a few wheat cakes and drink some hot tea. She slept well that night and by dawn, when they began the day's journey, was almost back to normal.

But the next few days took their toll and by the time they reached Erfoud Katherine was exhausted. They delayed in the town only long enough for Rashid to go to the bank and get money enough to pay the drivers and send some back to the nomad camp. As soon as he had done that he sent telegrams to Wade Contney at the embassy, to Jamal and to his grandfather, and telephoned his home. Then he hired a taxi for the trip to his oasis.

Two hours later Katherine was soaking in a tub of scented water, her clean hair wrapped in a towel, a glass of cold orange juice within reach. Every bone in her body ached. She didn't remember ever having been so tired.

As soon as she had her bath she slipped into one of the lacy nightgowns in the drawer and climbed into bed. When Fatima urged her to eat she said, "Tomorrow," and closing her eyes went promptly to sleep.

She was still tired when she woke the next morning. She felt slightly nauseous and was unable to eat even though Fatima looked at her with pleading eyes and tried to urge the food on her.

A few minutes after she'd sent Fatima away Rashid came into her room.

"What is it?" he asked. "Fatima said you wouldn't eat. Are you ill?"

"My stomach is still rocking from that rotten animal. I'll be all right tomorrow."

"Are you sure? Perhaps I'd better have a doctor flown in from Rabat."

"Rashid, really! I'm perfectly all right. It was a long hot trip and I'm exhausted, that's all." She sat up and pulled the satin sheet over her breasts. "When are we going back to Rabat?"

"I thought we might do it this afternoon. But now I think we should delay it until you feel better." He hesitated, not quite meeting her eyes. "I don't suppose a few days will make any difference now."

"No, I don't suppose so."

He sat beside her on the bed. "It's been a difficult time for you, Katherine. I've interfered with your life and I know I had no right to do that. I'm trying to set things straight now, so I went into Erfoud last night and telephoned your parents."

Katherine sat up in bed, her eyes wide. "What did you tell them?"

"That you had been my house guest. That we'd taken the jeep and gotten lost in a storm and that for the past three weeks we've been staying at an oasis. I assured them you were all right and would call them as soon as you had rested."

"What did they say?"

"They'd been out of town for part of that time, visiting your aunt in Portland, so they hadn't been aware you were missing. When they found out what had happened your father said I was a reckless son of a bitch to have gotten you into a situation like that and that I should be horsewhipped. Your mother cried. I offered to send them round-trip tickets to Casablanca and your father said he'd discuss that after he talked to you. I think I like him." A muscle jumped in his cheek. "I know that if a man did to my daughter what I've done to you I'd kill him."

"It's over now," Katherine said in a quiet voice. "Nothing is all bad, Rashid. There were good times too. Times I'll never forget—the sunsets, Abdur, Zahira."

And you, she wanted to add. I'll never forget you, Rashid, or the times I have laid in your arms. I'll never forget the passion we shared or the touch of your hand reaching for mine in the night.

She looked at him, wondering what he'd say if she told him how she felt. If she said I love you. I don't want to leave you. I'll be your mistress if you still want me. I'll be anything you want me to be, only don't send me away, Rashid. Don't send me away, my love.

But she couldn't say the words because she knew that even though she loved him, she couldn't live the kind of life she'd have to live as his mistress. And that when the day came—as it surely would—when he sent her away, she would not be able to bear it.

"It'll be all right. About my parents, I mean. I'll call them from Rabat."

"You'd better call Jamal too." He took a deep

breath. "I tried to phone him but he'd left Lyon. I imagine he's on his way back to Rabat."

Jamal. She'd have to face Jamal. She'd have to tell him. . . .

Suddenly the room spun out of focus.

"What is it?" She heard the sharp alarm in Rashid's voice. "Katherine, are you all right?" Strong arms eased her back against the pillows.

"Dizzy," she managed to whisper. "I'm so tired."

"Then sleep. I'll sit here with you."

"No, I'm okay, really."

But he took her hand and said, "Close your eyes, Katherine. I'll be right here."

Rashid sat beside her for a long time after she fell asleep. There were smudges of fatigue under her eyes and faint lines around her mouth. Her fair hair, bleached almost white by the sun, spread like a fan around her pale face. She'd lost weight these past few weeks. Her body looked fragile and delicate and he remembered how he had used it. He remembered the times he'd plunged into her with anger, when his hands had bruised her fair skin. He remembered the other times too, when her body had lifted to his with need and her soft hands had tightened on his shoulders and she'd cried his name.

He put his head down on the bed, near to the curve of her hip so that he could feel her warmth. "Katherine," he whispered over and over again. "Oh, Katherine."

Although Katherine was better the next day, Rashid insisted she stay in bed. That night Fatima placed a table on the balcony so that while they ate they could watch the sun set over the desert.

"I can understand now why you have a home here," she said. "There are times, like now, when everything is so incredibly lovely."

"It's been my special place where I could retreat from the world. But I don't think I want to stay here now. I may sell it."

"Sell it!" Katherine's eyes widened in disbelief. "But you love it here."

"Not anymore, Katherine. Things . . . things change. We change."

They ate the rest of the meal in silence and when they had finished Rashid said, "Would you like to take a walk around the oasis?"

"Of course. It's a lovely night."

The village, like the nomad camp, was quiet this time of evening. A million stars shone through the palms and the air was rich with the scent of the desert.

"You mustn't sell the house, Rashid," Katherine said. "These people depend on you."

"Someone else would take my place." He hesitated. "You have to know how to walk away when something is finished."

When they went in he took her to her door and said, "Tomorrow I'll arrange for the plane. We'll leave after lunch. I'm sure you'll feel better by then."

"Yes, I'm sure I will." Her voice was as formal as his.

But when she went into the room she closed the door and leaned against it for a long moment before she turned on the light. She felt empty, overcome by a sadness that was too deep for tears.

After she undressed and slipped into a pale yellow satin gown with a lace and ribbon-trimmed bodice, she sat in front of the dressing table to brush her hair and pat moisturizer on her sun-dried face. Finally she opened one of the bottles of French perfume and dabbed it behind her ears and in the hollow of her throat. When she sniffed her wrist she looked at her reflection in the mirror and murmured, "You smell delicious, kid." And could not understand the sudden tears that welled.

When the light was off she went out onto her balcony so that she could look out at the night and smell the sweet scent of the desert. When she heard a noise she turned. Rashid, dressed in a fresh white djellaba, stood shadowed in the doorway.

"I swore that I wouldn't come to you tonight," he said in a low voice. "But I couldn't help myself, Katherine. I had to be with you this one last time."

Wordlessly Katherine moved toward him. When she was close enough so that he could see her by the light from the corridor he said, "The gown matches your eyes. My grandfather was in love with a woman with yellow eyes a long time ago. He told me that when she was angry her eyes would narrow, the way yours narrow when you tell me you hate me."

He reached out and smoothed the hair back from her face. "But my grandfather was able to tame his yellow-eyed woman. I haven't been able to tame you, have I?"

"No," Katherine whispered, feeling the bumpy beat of her heart. "And now you never will."

"Won't I?" He scooped her up in his arms and carried her to the bed. When he pulled the gown over her head and took off his djellaba he leaned over her, and when he touched her he saw that she was trembling. "Are you still afraid of me?" he asked.

"I've always been afraid of you."

"I never wanted to hurt you, Katherine. But I wanted you . . . wanted you for my own." He kissed her gently. "When you look at me the way you're looking now, when I touch you and feel your body tremble under my hands, I feel like a king. I feel as though I'm going to live forever."

"Rashid . . ."

"Stay here with me, Katherine. Let me take care of you. Let me give you all the things I want to give you."

"Darling, please."

"Don't leave me, Katherine." His mouth crushed hers as he pulled her into his arms. It was a kiss that asserted his possession, his domination, and when he let her go he said, "You belong to me! You're mine!"

She waited, waited for him to say one word of love. When he didn't she said, "No, Rashid, I belong to myself."

"Can you deny what you feel? The way your body responds to mine?"

"No. No, I don't deny that. What we have is . . . is a special kind of magic. But it isn't enough. I can't be your mistress, Rashid. I don't want Parisian clothes or jewels. I don't want an apartment in Casablanca that you'll visit whenever it happens to be convenient for you."

"It wouldn't be like that," he protested.

But Katherine shook her head. "I'm not the woman for you, Rashid. Can you honestly picture me sitting in the background of your life, pouring mint tea for your guests, never opening my mouth to give an opinion?

Can you imagine me wearing a veil? Or being hidden from your family and business associates?" She shook her head. "I'm sorry, Rashid, but I'm worth more than that."

He let her go and his hands were shaking. "Damn it, Katherine, I won't let you go like this."

"You have to, Rashid." She tried to smile. "But we have tonight." Then, before he could speak again she covered his mouth with hers.

With a low groan Rashid clasped her to him and rolled her under him as his mouth claimed hers. He trailed a line of fire to her ear, tasting the skin behind it before he moved slowly down her neck to her shoulder. He took her hands, sniffing the perfumed wrists, touching them with his tongue before he took each of her fingers in his mouth to delicately suck.

When she put her arms around him to draw him up to her he said, "Lie still," and pushed her back against the satin pillows.

"If this is all we're going to have," he said in a hoarse voice, "if this is the last time, then I'm going to do all the things I've said I'd do to you. I'm going to have my fill of you, Katherine. When I've finished you can go back to Rabat or Maine or Princeton or any other damn place you want to go, but you'll carry the feel of my hands and my body on yours. You'll remember the taste of my mouth and that you cried my name in the darkness of the desert."

He crushed the lips that opened to protest, crushed them until they softened and yielded. His tongue tasted every corner of her mouth and her lips. At last he left her trembling mouth and, cupping both her breasts, began to kiss first one then the other, kiss them until her body quivered with a pleasure so exquisite it was almost painful. With featherlight touches his tongue flicked again and again against the rosy peaks.

"Touch me," he rasped. "Touch me." And moaned aloud as her fingers traveled down his body to caress him.

Katherine pressed her body to his, as excited as he was now. The waiting was torture and she whispered his name, urging him to come to her eager body. But he held her arms pinned to her sides when she reached for him again, not allowing her to move or touch him while his mouth devoured her breasts. When she cried out in protest he moved down her stomach to her thighs, taking small love bites, while Katherine, almost beside herself with need, whispered his name in an anguish of ecstasy. She gasped when his mouth found her secret core.

"No, it's too much," she said, trying to escape from the hands that held her, from the velvet tongue that drove her closer and closer to the brink of ecstatic desperation.

"No," she said again, even as her body yearned to his and she throbbed with a need so fierce she didn't think she could bear it. Then it was too much and as his hands tightened on her body she cried out, shuddering against him, struggling to free herself, her body pulsating with reaction as he touched her again and again.

"Darling, please, please no more," she cried, and at last he let her go and moved his body over hers.

He looked down into her yellow-smoke eyes, at the lips that were swollen with love. Then, with his gaze still locked to hers, he grasped her hips and entered her.

His body tight to hers, his legs holding her pinned and close, he moved feverishly against her. Head thrown back, the cords of his neck strained with the effort to slow the fires of his passion, he demanded another response.

"Again," he insisted, his body wild against hers as his fingers reached to grasp her peaked breasts. "Again, Katherine!"

She was lost, lost in a churning maelstrom of desire, crying his name again and again as her body peaked and trembled in shuddering surrender when he collapsed against her and cried his cry against her lips.

A long time passed before he eased his body from hers. He pulled her into his arms and after a while said, "There are love affairs that last longer than some marriages, Katherine."

Her body tensed. Again she waited, waited for one word of love.

He kissed her forehead. "We'd have such a wonderful time together, sweetheart. We could travel. You could have anything you wanted for as long as you wanted."

The words went on as he talked about things. The things he would give her. The things a man gave to his mistress. She turned her face away so that he wouldn't see her tears and when she was in control she said, "I'm sorry, Rashid. But no, the answer is still no."

His arms tightened around her and there was an edge of anger in his voice when he said, "How can you deny what's between us?"

"I don't deny it, but it isn't the way I want to live."

"That's final?"

"Final."

He didn't speak again and after a while she drifted to sleep. She woke abruptly when he lifted her out of bed and carried her toward the bathroom.

"Where are we going?" she whispered sleepily against his shoulder.

"I'm going to bathe you," he said as he pushed open the door. The room was filled with scented steam as he lowered her down into the big turquoise tub.

The warm water felt wonderful against her skin, as wonderful as the arms that still held her. When Rashid let her go he knelt in front of her and, taking the French soap in his hands, began to lather her body with it.

Katherine twisted her hair up into a knot, not sure whether to be amused or embarrassed by Rashid's attentions. It suddenly occurred to her that for the first time in her life she was actually proud of her body. Perhaps she wasn't too tall or too thin after all. Perhaps her breasts weren't too small. Next to Rashid she felt small and feminine and knew it was because that was the way he treated her. She wanted to throw herself into his arms and say, All right! All right, all right, I'll be your mistress. I'll be anything you want me to be because I love you. But she couldn't.

He took her arms, rubbing his soapy hands over them, up to her shoulders, down to her breasts. Gently he soaped them, drawing the suds out to the tips, then flicking the lather away.

"Give me the soap," Katherine said.

He shook his head. "No, I want to bathe you."

"And I want to bathe *you*." She reached for another bar and unwrapped it, then dipped the soap into the water and began to scrub his chest. She tangled her fingers in his chest hair, making little whirlygigs and curls before she trailed the suds down his stomach. Very softly she caressed his manhood with her soapy hands, looking at him with serious sad eyes.

He put his hand behind her neck and eased her closer so that he could kiss her lips.

When they came out of the tub he wrapped her in a big soft towel and dried her. Then he picked her up and carried her back to bed. They made love wordlessly, each gentle with the other, and when it was over Rashid said, "Sleep now. In the morning I'll make arrangements for the plane."

Then he kissed her forehead and said, "Good night, Katherine."

"Goodbye, Rashid," she said, her eyes filling with tears.

Chapter 14

FATIMA RETURNED THE CLOTHES KATHERINE HAD ARRIVED in, as well as the suitcase she had packed when she believed she was going to Marrakesh. It seemed odd, after more than a month of wearing caftans and djellabas, to dress in a skirt and blouse and high-heeled pumps.

The Berber woman, who had been weeping most of the morning, hovered over her. Every time Katherine tried to speak to her Fatima began to sob anew. She insisted on helping Katherine pack, but when she began taking the underwear and gowns out of the drawer Katherine stopped her.

"No," Katherine said, pointing to the clothes in her suitcase. "I'm only taking the clothes I brought with me."

Fatima threw up her hands, opened the closet doors and pointed to the caftans and rows of shoes.

Katherine shook her head and snapped the suitcase closed. "That's all there is, Fatima." She handed her the bag and walked her to the door.

When she was alone she looked around the room for one last time. The bottles of perfume were lined up on the dressing table next to the comb and brush set with the initial *K*. Once she closed the door it would be as though she'd never been here. She doubled her fists and for a moment held them to her eyes. Then she went out and closed the door behind her.

The table had been set in the dining room. There was a bouquet of orange-red poppies between two heavy silver candlesticks. A pitcher of martinis stood on the sideboard.

When she entered Rashid said, "I thought you might like a drink before lunch."

Katherine nodded. "Yes, thank you, I would."

He poured the drinks into chilled martini glasses and handed one to her. "To your health," he said, like a polite stranger.

"This is delicious." Her face felt frozen; the hand holding the glass trembled.

"We can leave for Rabat right after lunch."

"Fine."

"Would you like another drink?"

"No, thank you."

"Then shall we eat?" He pulled out her chair and as he started around the table they heard the screech of brakes. Rashid said, "I can't imagine who that can be, but whoever it is can wait until we've . . ."

Loud voices came from the entrance. Rashid glanced at Katherine. "I'd better go see who it is," he said. "I'll just be a moment."

But before he could move a man's voice shouted, "Damn it, boy, wait a minute!" Then Jamal, with his grandfather two steps behind him, burst into the room. He looked from Katherine to Rashid. His handsome face was pale, his hands clenched at his sides.

For a moment Rashid stared at his brother and grandfather. "This is a surprise," he said. "We were about to have lunch. Would you care to join us?"

"You bastard! How dare you act as though nothing has happened?" Jamal shouted. Turning his back on Rashid he ran to Katherine and, gripping her shoulders, cried, "Are you all right, Kathy?"

"Yes . . . yes, Jamal. I'm fine."

"He hasn't harmed you? If he has I swear to Allah I'll kill him."

"Jamal, please . . ." She was so stunned and confused it was difficult to think.

"He tricked you into coming here, didn't he?" His hands tightened on her shoulders and when she didn't answer he shook her and repeated, "Didn't he?"

"Yes," Rashid said. "I tricked her. I told her you were in Marrakesh and that I'd fly her there to meet you."

Jamal thrust Katherine aside and with a snarl turned to his brother. But before he could speak his grandfather cut in.

"In the name of Allah, why?" the old man roared. "What were you thinking of? Are you saying you kidnapped Miss Bishop?"

Rashid's face was cold. "Yes, Grandfather."

"Damn you!" Jamal cried as he leapt at Rashid, grabbing him by his shirt, his face distorted with rage as he doubled his fist and drove it into Rashid's face.

Blood spurted from Rashid's mouth as he staggered back.

"Stop it!" Katherine cried.

But Jamal was past listening. He struck Rashid again and when his brother didn't strike back Jamal shouted, "Fight back, damn you. Fight back!"

Katherine gripped Youssef's arm. "Stop them! Please stop them!"

The old man's face was grim. "I can't," he muttered. "This is something they must settle themselves."

There was another terrible sound of flesh hitting flesh.

"Don't!" Katherine's scream filled the room. She clutched Jamal's shoulder, trying to pull him away from Rashid. "Leave him alone!" she cried.

Still gripping Rashid's shirt front, Jamal whirled on her. "After what he did to you?" He shoved her away, his face a twisted mask of rage, and grabbed one of the heavy silver candlesticks off the table. "I'll kill him!"

Youssef cried out, but before he could move Katherine grabbed Jamal's arm. "Jamal, don't!" she screamed. "I love him! I love him."

Jamal's hand froze in midair. His face went white, his mouth agape.

Katherine took the candlestick out of his trembling hand. "I'm sorry, Jamal. But it's true."

No one spoke. Rashid put his hand to his bloody face. His eyes were wide with shock. "Katherine," he whispered, then started toward her.

With a low cry she backed away from him and ran out of the room, down the corridor to the room she thought she'd left forever. She slammed the door and sat on the bed, her head in her hands, taking deep gulping breaths.

When the door opened she looked up and saw that it was Youssef. He crossed to her and rested a hand on her head. "Are you ill, daughter?" he asked.

Katherine shook her head, trying to fight back the tears that the kindness in his voice released. "It was so awful, Youssef. It was my fault, all of it."

"No, my dear, you're not to blame. Beauty isn't a fault, nor is love. I knew the first time I saw you that some day there would have to be something between you and Rashid. There was a feeling, an electricity in the air when the two of you were together."

"He didn't even like me then."

"Perhaps he didn't like you, Miss Katherine, but it was plain to see that he wanted you more than he'd ever wanted anything in his life."

"For his mistress," she said in a low voice.

"What's that?"

"He wanted me for his mistress, Youssef. That's why he brought me here. Oh, it was to get me away from Jamal too, that was part of it. Rashid doesn't believe that a marriage between a Moroccan and a foreigner is possible—not for Jamal, not for him."

"I see." The old man sat down on the bed beside her and took her hand. "He's seen my example, of course, so he thinks such a marriage couldn't possibly work."

Katherine nodded. "He doesn't love me," she said in a bitter voice. "Not the way I want to be loved." She got up and threw open the closet doors. "This is the way he loves me." She indicated the racks of caftans, the rows of jeweled slippers.

"My grandsons are idiots," he said. "If I were thirty years younger I'd take you away from both of them." He went to stand beside her and, putting a finger under her chin, lifted it and said, "I'm going to take you to Marrakesh where you can rest and get some color back in your cheeks, Miss Katherine. Then you can think about what you're going to do. Have you packed?"

"Yes, Fatima took my bag."

"You're not taking these things?"

Katherine shook her head.

When they reached the living room they saw Rashid sitting on one of the sofas, his head back, his eyes closed. When he heard them he opened his eyes, but before he could get to his feet his grandfather said, "I'm taking Katherine back to Marrakesh with me."

Rashid nodded. "I'd like to speak to her first."

Youssef turned to her. "Do you wish to speak to him, my dear?"

"Yes."

"Then I'll wait in the car."

Rashid motioned Katherine to sit beside him. His face had been cleaned. Patches covered the cuts but not the bruises.

"Are you all right, Rashid?"

"Yes, I'm all right."

"Where's Jamal?"

"He's in his room. I'll talk to him when he's calmer." He picked a stack of mail up off the table beside the sofa and after shuffling through it extracted a letter. "Not that it matters now," he said, "but this is a letter from a business associate of mine in Tangier. It came while we were in the desert." He hesitated, took a deep breath and said, "For several years now I've heard talk of a woman Jamal visits in Tangier."

Katherine looked at him, puzzled, wondering what in the world he was talking about.

"When you and Jamal announced your engagement I asked my associate to check on the woman." He handed the letter to Katherine. "You can read it later but I'll tell you what it says." He stopped and ran a nervous hand through his dark hair. "Katherine, Jamal is already married. He's been married for two years."

"Married!" Her eyes went wide with shock. "I don't believe you. He was going to marry me."

"Of course he was. And if he had it would have been perfectly legal."

"But—"

"Have you forgotten that Moroccan men are allowed four wives?"

She stared at him in disbelief. "I would have been number two," she said after a moment.

"Jamal loves you, Katherine. In his own way he loves you."

"Yes, I suppose he does." She stood up. "But it doesn't matter now. Whatever there was between Jamal and me was finished a long time ago."

"What about us, Katherine?"

"There is no us, Rashid."

"You said you loved me."

"I do." She swallowed, then bravely met his gaze. "That makes me a special kind of a fool, doesn't it?"

"Katherine." He put his hand on the side of her face. "I should have told you weeks ago that I loved you."

She moved away from his hand. "You don't have to say that, Rashid. I know how you feel about me."

"No, you don't. Didn't you hear what I just said? I love you, Katherine. I've loved you for a long time."

She shook her head, averting her eyes. With all her heart Katherine wished she could believe him. And perhaps he did love her—in his fashion. If she became his mistress she'd be well taken care of. She wouldn't want for anything and when it was over he'd very likely provide for her future—her future without him.

"Goodbye, Rashid," she said.

"I won't let you go!" But before he could touch her, his grandfather came through the front door. He looked from Katherine to Rashid. Then he put his arm protectively around her.

"I'm taking Miss Katherine out of here now," he said. "I'm taking her away from you."

"Damn it, Grandfather—"

"Don't try to stop me. You've done enough to this girl. If you ever hurt her again I'll have you horse-whipped."

"Katherine, I have to talk to you." Rashid's voice held a note of panic she'd never heard before.

She shook her head. "We've said it all." She leaned on Youssef's shoulder, trembling with fatigue and reaction. With one last look at Rashid she let his grandfather help her out to the waiting car.

The house in Marrakesh, with its ornately carved Moorish arches and sparkling clean tile floors, was a quiet haven of rest.

On the morning after her arrival Youssef placed a call to Katherine's mother and father in Buckport. After reassuring her parents that she was perfectly all right, she told them that her engagement to Jamal had been broken. Her mother, as she did with any startling news, immediately burst into tears. Her father said if that damn A-rab had done anything to hurt her he'd get on the first plane to Marrakesh and would thrash him within an inch of his life.

Katherine tried to cheer her mother up and told her father that it was she who had broken the engagement. She didn't add that Jamal already had a wife and she'd almost become number two.

It was still difficult to believe. Had Jamal really thought he could get away with such a deception? Hadn't he realized that someday she would have become suspicious? That once she had known she would have left him?

She knew now that she'd fallen out of love with Jamal years ago and that if it hadn't been for Rashid and wanting to show him that she wasn't a twenty-year-old who'd stand by and let him direct her life, she would never have agreed to marry Jamal.

She phoned Wade Contney and was informed by his secretary that Mr. Contney was unavailable. When she asked about the status of her job she was told that Mr. Contney had put her on a six-month leave of absence and that he had recommended her for a post in Somalia. Somalia? Wade must know she'd never accept the transfer. It seemed that her career in the foreign service was at an end.

With a wry grin she put the phone down, then picked it up and phoned a company in Geneva whose vice-president had approached her at an embassy party several months before about coming to work for them. The man was delighted she'd called and arranged an appointment with her on the first of October.

For now it was nice to rest and not think about anything. Youssef was a wonderful host. He insisted Katherine sleep as long as she could in the morning. When she woke she had only to ring her bedside bell and by the time she'd bathed her breakfast arrived. Youssef took her out to dinner almost every night, showed her everything there was to see in Marrakesh and constantly brought her presents.

"I can't accept this," Katherine said over and over.

"Nonsense, daughter. It's only a trinket. Give it to one of the servants if you don't like it."

Often they sat together out in the garden in the evening while he told her stories of his youth, of his sons and his grandsons.

"I lost my oldest boy, Hassan, when he was only twelve," Youssef said. "He was a wonderful boy, a good scholar, as loving a child as a parent could hope for. Brahim, Rashid and Jamal's father, was a good student too, but he was a little wild, a little unpredictable. He was killed in a car accident when my grandsons were young. By then my wife, Monique, was living in Paris. I kept the boys, Rashid and Jamal, with me every summer."

He looked at Katherine, his face thoughtful. "It was interesting, how different they were even then. As different as Hassan and Brahim had been. Jamal was a lot like his uncle Hassan. But I think Rashid was—and is—more like me."

Katherine smiled. "Yes, I think so too."

"You love him, do you?"

"Yes." She hesitated. "It happened so gradually, Youssef. I hated him for so long because of what he'd done years ago. Then, when he took me away to the desert, I thought it was only to separate Jamal and me again. When he told me he wanted me to be his mistress . . ."

"You escaped into the desert." His fierce dark eyes, so like Rashid's, looked into hers.

"That was only part of it. You see he had . . ." She felt hot color creep to her cheeks.

Youssef's mouth hardened. "I should have horse-whipped him that day I took you away."

Katherine shook her head. "It wasn't just Rashid, Youssef. I felt . . . I was so terribly attracted to him. But I couldn't accept the fact that I might be falling in love with a man I'd hated for seven years. And he's Jamal's brother—that's what made the way I felt so awful. So I ran away."

"Were you lovers at the nomad camp?" he asked in a gentle voice.

"Yes, Youssef. I know it's hard for you to understand, but sometimes love is beyond explanation."

"Is it really?" A slight smile curved his mouth. "Why is it that young people always think older people can't understand? Do you think we've never been young, that our bodies never burned with longing the way yours do?"

"No, of course not. I didn't mean that."

"There have been women in my life, daughter, but only one that I felt about as I think Rashid feels about you—Monique St. Onge, the woman who became my wife, who is still my wife."

Because it was a night for confidences, Katherine said, "Tell me about her."

"She's beautiful. I haven't lived with her for twenty years and I haven't seen her in eight, but I know she's still beautiful. She's small and blond, classically French."

Youssef leaned back in his chair, gazing out at the lights of Marrakesh below. "Morocco was a French protectorate until 1956, which is why almost all of us speak French. Monique's father was governor. I was in college then and I belonged to a group of student radicals who were determined to throw the French out of Morocco. My father, who wanted to get along with the French, didn't approve of my actions. Trying to convince me what fine people the French were, he insisted I go with him to a governor's reception, a garden party type of thing that was fashionable in those days.

"I didn't want to go, but one didn't argue with one's father back then. So I went, but I'm afraid I was unforgivably rude to everyone I talked to. Then I saw Monique."

Katherine leaned forward in her chair, her gaze on Youssef's face.

"She was springtime," he said simply. "Springtime in a green dress. She wore satin slippers and she carried a chiffon scarf that fluttered from her fingers each time she spoke." He looked away from Katherine, rubbing a gnarled hand across his face. After he cleared his throat, he turned back to her and with a forced smile said, "I was in love. Instantaneously, hopelessly, angrily in love."

"Angrily?"

"I hated the French and here I was enraptured by a French woman and I didn't know what to do about it. We were introduced and I think I said something rude because I remember that she raised one perfect eyebrow and turned away to speak to someone else. But as soon as she detached herself from a group I went up to her and said, 'I'd like to speak to you, mademoiselle.' "

He chuckled. "Her eyes cut right through me, daughter. She said, 'I can't imagine why, monsieur. It's obvious that you and I have nothing to say to each other.'

"So I took her arm and before she could say another word I waltzed her away from the reception to a small side garden that was hidden by a stand of willows. She struggled and sputtered and when we stopped I pulled her into my arms and kissed her."

"What did she say to that?"

"She didn't say anything. She just hauled off and hit me so hard my teeth rattled."

Katherine laughed. "Good for her! What did you do then?"

"I slapped her back." He held up a cautioning hand. "Before you say anything let me tell you that was the first and the last time I ever raised a hand to Monique. But you see I'd been raised thinking women were second-class citizens. Morocco was even more of a man's world back then than it is now. The idea of a woman striking a man was unheard of. It was a reflex action; I did it before I thought."

He chewed his lower lip, looking, it seemed to Katherine, like a very small boy who has just been caught with his hand in the cookie jar.

"What happened then?" she said.

"Monique started to cry. I looked at her, at that perfect white face with the imprint of my hand getting redder and redder, and I wanted to kill myself. I pulled her back into my arms. She struggled for a minute or two but I wouldn't let her go and after a little while she quieted down. We just stood there, daughter, me shaking like a leaf with her head against my shoulder. I kissed her again. I kissed her and kissed her because I knew then I'd never get enough of her.

"When I finally took her back to the party her father jumped all over me. I asked him if I could call on Monique and he said no. But I did anyway. He wouldn't let me see her so I waited until that night, hoping she might come out into the garden after dark. When she did I asked her to marry me."

"That fast?"

"That fast," he said with a smile. "Three days later we ran away. We took a boat to Cádiz, found a priest who'd marry us and made our way to Granada. We honeymooned there for a week and then we went to Venice." He leaned back in his chair, his eyes closed. "Spring blossomed into summer and we didn't want to leave; we wanted to float along the Grand Canal forever. It was the most wonderful time of my life, daughter. I'd die happy right now if I could relive just one hour of that precious time with Monique."

Katherine dared not interrupt him, but finally he opened his eyes and said, "It was difficult for her to adjust when we came back to Morocco. She was used to going about as she pleased and a woman simply didn't go out like that here—not back in those days. All of the Moroccan women were veiled then. Monique kept insisting she wasn't Moroccan, she was French, and I kept insisting that French or not, she was married to me and she'd live like a Moroccan woman."

"It must have been difficult for both of you."

"Difficult? It was impossible. If we hadn't been so in

love we'd have killed each other that first year of marriage. It was better after Monique got pregnant, but it was terrible for her when Hassan died. By the time Brahim went away to the university she was restless again. She wanted so desperately to be her own woman and I wanted just as desperately for her to be *my* woman."

He ran a hand through his shock of white hair. "Our differences finally became irreconcilable and she left me. That was almost twenty years ago."

"That's a long time, Youssef. A long time to be alone. Wasn't there—isn't there—some way the two of you could reconcile?"

"No." His face hardened. "I love Monique but I won't beg. If she ever comes back to me it'll be because she wants to, not because I ask her to."

"You've never thought of taking another wife?"

"Monique is my wife and she'll be my one and my only wife until the day I die."

For a long time they didn't speak, then in a quieter voice Youssef said, "You go in now, daughter. It's late."

"Can I get you anything, Youssef?"

"No, no, thank you. I just want to sit here for a little while."

"All right." But still Katherine hesitated. Youssef was such a strong man, yet at this minute he seemed so vulnerable, so lost. She put her hand on his shoulder, then kissed his cheek. Before he could speak she turned away, feeling as desolate as he felt now, wanting to weep for all lost loves.

Chapter 15

YOUSSEF KNOCKED ON KATHERINE'S DOOR THE NEXT morning when she was having breakfast. Without any preliminaries he said, "Rashid is here."

Coffee cup halfway to her mouth, Katherine stared at him. "Here?"

"He wants to speak to you, daughter. I told him it was up to you."

She put the cup back on the tray. "All right," she said at last. "I'll see him."

"You can use my study."

"Thank you, Youssef. Will you tell him please that I'll be down in half an hour?"

He nodded. "Are you sure you want to do this?"

"No, but I will."

She looked like an American when she came downstairs. Her blond hair had been pulled back off her face into a sleek chignon. She wore a short white cotton dress that buttoned down the front, and smart black and white high-heeled pumps. Although she didn't feel it, she knew she looked cool and controlled.

When she went into the library Rashid was standing near the fireplace, his back to the door. He swung around when she entered, his eyes warming at the sight of her.

"Good morning, Katherine."

"Good morning, Rashid. I hope I didn't keep you waiting."

"No, no, of course not." He crossed the room to her, and taking her arm led her to a sofa. "I have to talk to you, Katherine," he said. "You . . . you look lovely. I see that Youssef's been taking good care of you."

She nodded. "He's a wonderful man."

"Yes, he is. He's still angry with me. He raised absolute hell when I arrived. I didn't think he was even going to let me see you. He probably wouldn't have if I hadn't told him he was behaving like a Moroccan father and that the decision should be yours." He tapped long fingers on the coffee table in front of them. "I'm afraid it'll be a long time before either Jamal or I are back in his good graces."

"Where is Jamal now?"

"In Tangier." He pulled an envelope out of his breast pocket. "He asked me to give you this, Katherine. He also asked me to tell you how sorry he is that he didn't tell you he was married."

"It doesn't seem to matter now." She took the envelope and put it down on the table. "Poor Jamal. He just wanted to go back to the way things were. He wanted to be twenty-one again. And so did I, I suppose." She looked at Rashid. "Are things all right between the two of you?"

"Not yet, Katherine. But I think they will be."

"Is the . . . is the woman he's married to nice?"

"I don't know. I've never met her and I have no intention of meeting her."

"That's not fair, Rashid. Jamal is your only brother; his wife is a part of your family. Nothing that's happened has been her fault."

"Damn him! Why couldn't he have told you he was married? He knew once you found out you'd leave him. Why is he so weak?"

"Because you let him be weak," she said in a quiet voice. "You made all his decisions for him, Rashid. You never let him grow up."

His mouth tightened and Katherine could see the effort it took to control himself. Finally he said, "You're right, I suppose. He was eight years younger than I was and both his mother and father were dead. I loved him. I wanted to take care of him."

"It's time to let him go."

"I know." He got up abruptly. "But I didn't come here to talk about Jamal, Katherine. I came to talk about us."

"I told you the last time we were together that there isn't any us." Her mouth felt stiff when she tried to smile. "But I'll talk about me if you like. To begin with, I'm through at the embassy."

"What?"

"Wade wouldn't even talk to me."

"But I told him what happened! I told him I'd tricked

you, that I'd taken you away against your will and that we'd been lost in the desert for almost a month." He struck his fist against his palm. "I lost my temper but, damn it, I didn't think he'd hold that against you."

"What do you mean?"

"All I tried to do was make it clear that your being away wasn't your fault. He made some sly remark about my doing what he and every other man in Rabat had been wanting to do ever since you'd arrived from the States and that now maybe you'd be more accessible. I hit him. I'm sorry, Katherine, I couldn't help myself."

"That's all right." her mouth quirked in a smile. "I hope you gave him a shot for me. But now I know why he was having me transferred to Somalia."

"Somalia? My God! You're not going, are you?"

"No, I've resigned. I'm going back to Rabat in a few days to close up my apartment. Then I think I'll go to Europe for a while and play tourist. When I'm ready there's a company in Geneva that might take me on."

"Katherine . . ." He sank down on the sofa and took her hand in his. "I'm not going to let you go anywhere. You don't have your job to worry about now. I'm sorry about that, but I wouldn't have let you work once we were together anyway." He touched the side of her face and, clasping the back of her neck, drew her to him.

"Rashid . . ." Her voice held a warning note as she pulled away. "Can you hear yourself? Can you hear what you're saying? '*I'm* not going to let you go anywhere. *I* wouldn't have let you work once we were together.' You're trying to run my life."

"You love me—"

"Yes, I love you but I won't be . . . be *ruled!*"

His face tightened. "You're exaggerating. It wouldn't be like that."

"Wouldn't it?"

"I love you, Katherine."

"And I love you. But I can't live the way you want me to. I'm sorry. I—"

Before she could go on he pulled her into his arms and kissed her, a crushing, demanding kiss that spoke of both hunger and desire.

Her hands were flat against his chest and she could feel the frantic beat of his heart. "No," she whispered as the silken moistness of his tongue invaded her mouth and he pushed her back against the pillows, his arms sliding around her back to draw her closer.

"Katherine," he said against her lips. "I love you, I love you."

His hands fumbled with the buttons of her dress and she tried to pull away from him, tried even when he touched the fullness that strained over the top of her lacy bra.

"They've grown," he whispered as he rubbed his face against her breasts. "Are you gaining weight, my love?"

"Rashid, don't. I don't want to do this. I don't want to start . . ."

But he had pulled the lace aside, exposing her breasts to his hands and his mouth. The rosy nipples were swollen and waiting as his hands cupped her. He took first one then the other in his mouth, nibbling as though they were grapes, rolling them around on his tongue before he began to suckle.

Katherine was frantic with fear that Youssef or one of

the servants would come in. But her body, aching with desire, arched to his and her fingers fastened in the thickness of his hair, holding him there, poised over her breasts.

Morning sunlight flooded the room, turning her skin to gold, the hands that caressed her to bronze.

She was not aware her dress had slid up until she felt Rashid's hand cup her through the filmy panties.

"No," she whispered, trying to pull away from him. "No, don't."

His fingers lifted the lacy elastic and reached to caress her. "I want you," he whispered. "I want you now." His hand was warm against her flesh.

"No!" she cried as she pulled away and frantically tried to straighten her clothes. "I won't let you start this again. I'm not going to be your mistress. I've told you—"

"All right." His voice was hoarse. "All right, damn it, I'll marry you."

"What did you say?"

"I said I'd marry you. Whenever you want. Now. Today. I don't care if it's a Moslem or a Christian ceremony. I'll do whatever you want to do, but I won't let you go."

Katherine looked at him, then slowly she pulled away and, leaning back against the sofa, closed her eyes. Finally she looked at him and said, "You don't really want to marry me, Rashid. You've offered to because you know marriage is the only thing I'll settle for."

"What difference does it make? The idea of marriage may take some getting used to for me, but if that's what you want, if that's the only way I can have you, then I'm willing to marry you."

"I see. Well thank you, but I don't want a man who's 'willing to marry me.'" She got to her feet and offered him her hand. "Goodbye, Rashid," she said in a barely controlled voice.

He looked at her, his face tortured with uncertainty. "You can't just . . . just throw us away. We can work things out if you'll give it a chance. I'll do whatever you want. I'll—"

But when Katherine shook her head his face hardened and he said, "I tried to force you once. I'll never do that again. And I won't beg. If you change your mind you'll have to come to me."

She stared down at her trembling hands, fighting to keep herself from crying out. She didn't look up when she heard him cross the room, open, then close the door.

Three days later Katherine took the train to Rabat. She packed the things she wanted to keep and had them shipped back to the States. She gave a large cocktail party, inviting the friends and acquaintances she'd made since she'd been in Morocco so she could tell them all goodbye at the same time.

"Contney is a real bum," her secretary, Alice McGoverty, said. "Everybody at the embassy hates the way he treated you."

"It doesn't matter now," Katherine said as she refilled Alice's glass.

It really didn't. She'd said her farewells; it was time to move on.

She wrote to her parents to tell them she was leaving Morocco and that she'd write from Madrid or Paris.

The day before she left she telephoned Youssef to say goodbye.

"If you change your mind and decide to come back here," he said, "you always have a home with me in Marrakesh."

"Thank you, Youssef. Thank you for everything."

"Where will you go first, daughter?"

"Madrid, I think. Then probably Paris."

"If you go to Paris I'd appreciate it if you'd call on Monique. Would you mind?"

"No, of course not. Any message?"

"No, no message. Do you have enough money?"

Katherine smiled into the phone. "Yes, Youssef. Please don't worry?"

"You'll write?"

"Of course I'll write."

"You'll come back someday. I know you will."

"Perhaps."

Perhaps. But she wouldn't. This part of her life had finished. She knew she was like a toy Rashid wanted and would do anything to get—and she knew she couldn't live like that. But she was equally certain she had to get away before she lost all of her pride and her hardwon sense of right and wrong—and accepted Rashid on his own terms . . . on any terms.

Chapter 16

THE HOUSE AT NUMBER 28, RUE ST. CROIX DE LA
Bretonnerie, was a narrow two-story brownstone that
reminded Katherine of old New York apartments.
Orange and yellow marigolds sided the flagstone entrance, and windowboxes, filled with bright red gerani-
ums, decorated each front window.

On the telephone that morning Monique St. Onge
had sounded pleasant but reserved.

"I've just come from Morocco," Katherine had said.
"Youssef Ben Hasir asked me to phone to say hello."

"How nice. How is Youssef?"

"He's quite well."

"And the boys, Jamal and Rashid?"

"They're fine."

"Are you enjoying Paris?"

"I've only been here a few days. But yes, thank you,
it's a lovely city."

Polite, forced conversation. Finally the polite, forced invitation to tea.

Had she come out of curiosity to see this French woman who was Youssef's wife? Katherine wondered as she lifted the knocker. Or because she was lonesome? For the past month she'd had no one to talk to except hotel desk clerks and waiters. She longed to sit down and talk to someone, someone who knew Youssef and Rashid.

Summer had ended and already there was the hint of autumn in the air. On the way to visit Monique, Katherine had walked down the Champs Elysées, admiring the smartly dressed and coiffed women, the shops and the restaurants, trying to recapture the wonderful feeling she'd had on other visits to Paris. But the magic was gone; she was alone and depressed. She could feel the chilly threat of the winter that was to come.

The gray silk dress she wore matched her mood. Cut of classic lines, it had a high neck and long sleeves. Her shoes and bag matched the dress. She wore her hair pulled back into a bun. She knew she looked dignified, proper enough to meet this Frenchwoman who had sounded so coolly remote on the telephone. One cup of tea, Katherine told herself, a few comments about Youssef and that's it.

The woman who opened the door was in her late sixties. Her face, as smooth as that of a woman half her age, still had the gamine look that only French women carry off so well. Her hair, a lovely soft white, was fashionably short. She wore a light blue dress and carried a blue chiffon scarf.

Before she thought, Katherine said, "Youssef told

me you were carrying a chiffon scarf the first time he saw you. He said it was green, to match your dress."

Delicate eyebrows raised and the mouth that had looked severe before softened. "I always hold a scarf when I'm nervous. It gives me something to do with my hands." Monique St. Onge opened the door wider. "You must be Miss Bishop. Please come in."

She led Katherine through a foyer into one of the most charming rooms Katherine had ever seen, a room that seemed to reflect the woman herself. The wallpaper was pale blue, the thick carpeting a deeper blue. The furniture was polished and gleaming. A vase of pink roses adorned a table that had been set for tea under the windows.

"Would you like a glass of sherry?" Monique said as she led Katherine to a chair. "Or would you prefer something stronger?"

"Sherry would be nice, thank you."

When Monique had poured it from a crystal decanter on the coffee table in front of them, she handed a glass to Katherine and said, "How long will you be in Paris?"

"I'm not sure. A week or two. Maybe longer."

"Are you on vacation?"

"In a way. I'm between jobs. I had been working at the United States Embassy in Rabat. There's a job waiting for me in Geneva. I have an interview there the first of October."

"Then you'll have plenty of time to enjoy Paris." Monique set the glass of sherry on the table in front of her. "How long have you known Youssef and my grandsons?"

"I've only known Youssef for a few months. I met

Jamal a little over seven years ago when we were at Princeton."

The blue eyes widened. *"Alors!* Then you are the girl he was so crazy about! He stayed with me when he came back from the United States, while he attended the Sorbonne. For months he was desolate. He spoke of nothing else. But he was young—you were both young." She gave a delicate Gallic shrug. "I'm sure you recovered. Have you seen him recently?"

"Yes, madame, quite recently. We were engaged a few months ago but the engagement has been broken."

"I see." The blue eyes looked at her quizzically.

Katherine lowered her gaze, pretending to study the glass she held so tightly in her hand. In the silence of the room she could hear the ticking of the clock that stood in the foyer.

"Well, shall we have our tea?" Monique rose and led Katherine to the table.

Mon Dieu, Monique thought, social amenities were a bore. Why was it that just because you lived in Paris everyone who has ever known you feels free to give your telephone number to friends and relatives? But of course Youssef had been—and still was—more than just someone she'd known. Besides, in all the time she'd lived in Paris this was the first time he'd ever asked someone to phone her.

"Youssef is well?" she asked.

"He's fine. He's a remarkable man."

"Yes, he is." A slight smile crossed Monique's face. "Is he as handsome as ever?"

"I don't know how he looked before, but yes, he's handsome. And dynamic. He's been kind to me, madame. I've grown very fond of him."

"Have you met Rashid?"

"Yes."

"You know it's odd, but I'd have thought you and Rashid far more suited than you and Jamal." She saw color creep into the young woman's face and looked at her a bit more closely. This Miss Bishop was rather interesting. She was absolutely stunning, of course. Her clothes were good, although a bit serious for someone her age, as was her coiffeur. She seemed poised and well mannered, but rather obviously unhappy.

Monique suppressed a sigh. She'd offer tea and sandwiches but she was all out of sympathy, particularly for young Americans who might prove to be a nuisance. She'd be pleasant and patient and with good luck this Miss Bishop wouldn't linger.

"Have a bit of pâté," she said. "The caviar is good too, if you have a taste for it."

"Yes, I'm fond of caviar." Katherine took a bite of the salty black delicacy and felt her stomach lurch. She stared at her plate, not knowing whether to keep on chewing or to swallow and get it over with. She swallowed, then took a sip of tea, willing her stomach to behave.

"Have you been to the Louvre?" Monique asked. "I understand there's a special exhibition this month that—"

"I beg your pardon." Katherine pushed her chair back. "I wonder if I might use your bathroom?"

"Of course." The delicate eyebrows climbed. "Just down the hall, second door on your left."

Katherine, whose teeth were clenched, only nodded, trying not to run as she crossed the dark blue carpet to the hall. By sheer force of will she made it to the bathroom before she was ill.

When she was able, she rinsed her mouth, splashed cold water on her face and smoothed the random strands of hair dampened by perspiration. Her hands tightened around the cool porcelain sink as she looked at herself in the mirror. Her face was pale and there were dark smudges beneath her eyes.

She forced herself to take deep breaths. Youssef's wife must think I'm an idiot, she thought. I'd have been all right if it hadn't been for that caviar. Oh sweet heaven, don't think about the caviar.

Monique looked up inquiringly when Katherine returned to the table. "Are you all right?" she asked politely. "You look a bit pale."

"Traveling always upsets me. The change in the water, I suppose."

"The water? Are you sure that's all it is?"

"Yes, madame, quite sure."

"Let me pour you a hot cup of tea. That will help." She studied Katherine as the young woman sipped her tea, and when finally Katherine said, "I really must be going. Thank you for tea," Monique breathed a sigh of relief.

But when they stood at the door there was something about Katherine that touched her. The young woman was so obviously alone, and Paris was not a kind city to be alone in. So she said, "I'm having a small dinner party tomorrow night, Miss Bishop. Won't you please come?"

"Thank you, madame, but—"

"Please, my dear. I insist. It's a small party, very

informal. To tell you the truth, I'm short a woman. You'd really be doing me a great favor."

"Yes, all right," Katherine said. "Thank you for asking me."

Monique watched her go down the flagstone walk. At the gate Katherine turned and waved, a bit hesitantly, and Monique waved back. Now why in the world did I invite her? she wondered. She's apt to ruin a perfectly good party.

It was a good party, and Katherine didn't ruin it. She looked charming in a pink wool dress of softly flattering lines. Her light hair had been pulled back off her face and done in a cascade of curls. Her only jewelry was a thin gold bracelet and matching earrings she'd bought in Marrakesh.

The other guests, once they realized she spoke excellent French, were friendly. Three of the men tried to sit next to her at dinner and later asked if they might have the pleasure of showing her Paris. To each of them she said, *"Merci,* but no thank you."

Monique watched Katherine with growing approval. When it came time for the guests to leave she put her hand on Katherine's arm and in a low voice said, "Stay a bit, will you?"

After Monique said her farewells she came back into the living room where Katherine was and sighed. "I love to have company but I also love it when they leave. Let's have a brandy, shall we?"

"Are you sure? You must be tired. I'd be glad to help you straighten up."

"My maid will be here in the morning. I'm going to be an absolute wretch and leave the mess for her."

Monique swirled the brandy gently, warming the glass between her hands. In a carefully casual voice she asked, "Are you feeling better than you were yesterday?"

"Yes, thank you."

"Do you still think it was the water? I'm surprised you don't drink bottled water."

"Yes, well . . . well perhaps it was something else."

Monique put the snifter of brandy on the table. "I had two children, Miss Bishop," she said gently. "It was a long time ago but I still remember how a woman looks when she's pregnant."

Every bit of color drained out of Katherine's face.

"You are pregnant, aren't you? Is the child Jamal's?"

Katherine's hands tightened around the crystal glass. "No, madame."

"*Mon Dieu*, will you stop calling me madame? My name is Monique and I'd like to be your friend." She reached across the table and took Katherine's hand. "Now what do you mean the child isn't Jamal's? You were engaged to him. Has he run out on you because you're pregnant?"

Katherine shook her head. "We broke the engagement because I'm not in love with Jamal. After I broke it I found out that he already has a wife. But that really has nothing to do with it and it's just . . . just not important." Freeing her hand she got to her feet. "I'm really very tired. I enjoyed your party and thank you for asking me."

"Sit down!" the older woman snapped. "Now, please, finish your brandy and then I'll phone for a taxi. You'll never find one on the street at this hour and Youssef would never forgive me if I let anything happen to you. Apparently he's taken you under his wing and I think there must be a very good reason for this. Was he aware when you left Morocco that you were pregnant?"

"No, I didn't know myself. I thought it was the effects of the heat, of being lost in the desert for such a long time."

"Lost in the desert! *Mon Dieu,* what are you talking about?"

Katherine ran a tired hand across her face. "It's an awfully long story and it really is very late."

"Then why don't you spend the night? Look, *chérie,* I've got an extra bedroom. Let me give you a gown and make sure you're comfortable. We can talk in the morning."

"That's kind of you, but I really should get back to the hotel."

"Nonsense." Monique got to her feet. "You mustn't run around Paris alone at this hour, not when I have a perfectly good guest room. Come along, I'm an old lady and it upsets me to have people argue with me."

It was easier to acquiesce. Katherine followed Monique St. Onge into the guest room, accepted a nightgown and robe and a pat on the head.

In a strange way it felt good to have someone know about her pregnancy. She'd been telling the truth when she said she hadn't known about it when she left Morocco. Perhaps it was just as well she hadn't because she wasn't sure she would have had the courage to have said no to Rashid if she'd known she was carrying his child. There had been times these last few weeks when she had wanted to pick up a telephone and call him. But she'd been afraid, afraid that if he knew he'd come after her—and she wouldn't have the strength to say no to him again.

She placed her hands over her stomach. Rashid's child. She carried Rashid's child. Sooner or later she'd have to make a decision—not a decision about whether or not she'd have the baby. Of course she'd have it. But she had to decide whether or not to stay in Europe, what to tell the firm in Geneva and how she'd break the news to her parents. She still remembered her mixed feelings of joy and chagrin when the doctor in Madrid told her she was pregnant. She still felt a bit that way but in her heart she knew everything would be all right. She'd have her baby and she'd raise it. And every time she looked at him, for surely it would be a boy, she'd see a part of Rashid. A part of him would always be with her.

"Incredible!" Monique said when Katherine finished recounting all that had happened to her since she'd first arrived in Morocco. Her blue eyes were wide with shock. "Do you mean to say that Rashid carried you away to that place of his, not only with the idea of getting you away from Jamal but of keeping you for himself?"

Katherine nodded and took a croissant from the breakfast cart Monique had wheeled into her room a few minutes earlier. "Yes, madame." She bit her lip and smiled. "Monique."

"The scoundrel! How dare he be so high-handed? Carrying you off to the desert like some modern-day sheik. Barbaric! Oh, that boy! I could throttle him!" She pushed her chair back and began to pace up and down the room, blue dressing gown swishing behind her. "I love Rashid. He has great strength of character. But he had to grow up too fast and perhaps that's part of his problem. He became a man before he had the opportunity to be a boy."

She sat down and took a sip of coffee. "Perhaps if he'd had a more caring mother things might have been different. But Nadia was a difficult woman and when my son took another wife she never forgave him—or Rashid—even though Rashid was only a small boy. She turned away from him and lost herself in a world of veiled women while Rashid struggled on alone.

"Morocco is so much of a man's world, Katherine. I sometimes think that men there need lessons on how to deal with women. They're so used to bulldozing their way in their world of men that when they fall in love they use the same tactics with women, as Rashid did with you."

She thumped her small fist against the table. "Men need to be taught tenderness. I doubt that Rashid ever had anyone tell him that most women like to be persuaded into love. He's never been tamed, Katherine. It's too bad you left him because I rather think you're the one woman who could have done the job."

Katherine tried to smile. "With a chair in one hand and a whip in the other?"

"No, my dear, with love, tenderness and a great deal of patience."

Trying to change the subject, Katherine said, "What about Jamal's mother? What was she like?"

"Zohra was a lovely girl from one of the Berber villages near the Sahara. She wasn't happy in either Casablanca or Marrakesh. I remember her as always being sick. When my son Brahim died she was too distraught to take hold of things. I wish now that I could have helped her, but by that time I was living in Paris."

Delicate, well-manicured hands raised the cup to her lips. "I suppose you wonder why I left Youssef and live in Paris."

"He said it was difficult for you in Morocco."

"Difficult! It was impossible! I couldn't go out alone and I could only rarely go out with him. My time was supposed to be spent with other women or my children. If Youssef had guests for dinner I couldn't be present. The only time I could be myself was at night when we finally closed the bedroom door on the rest of the world. That's the only time Youssef acted like the man I'd fallen in love with."

"Things have changed there a bit now," Katherine said. "There are more women at the universities and more professional women. But it's still difficult. I know that I wouldn't be able to cope with it."

"Even if you loved Rashid?"

"Even if I . . ." Katherine's voice broke. "Even if I loved him," she said in a low voice.

"Do you love him, *chérie?*"

Katherine bowed her head, pinching the bridge of her nose between her thumb and forefinger. "Yes," she said in a muffled voice. "Yes, I love him."

"Then don't you think you ought to tell him you're pregnant? I'm sure if he knew he'd forget that nonsense about your being his mistress and marry you."

"He's already asked me to marry him, Monique."

"*Alors?* Then there is no problem."

"Isn't there? Rashid's proposal, which went something like 'All right, damn it, I'll marry you,' was offered in the heat—if that's the right word—of the moment. He doesn't really want to get married."

"But my dear Katherine, there's not a man alive who *wants* to get married. Ninety-nine percent of the married men walking around today aren't quite sure how it happened. Almost all of them, given their way, would never have taken the step. If you'd had the sense you were born with you'd have snapped up Rashid's proposal, such as it was, and dragged him, kicking and screaming, to the nearest priest."

"I have a perfect mental vision of that," Katherine said with a laugh. "I wish it were that easy, Monique, but it isn't. There are so many things to think about, so many things to consider. Rashid is a strong man, a man determined to have his own way. And I'm used to making my own decisions, to being my own woman."

Her forehead wrinkled in a frown as she tried to explain. "Don't you see, it's not just Rashid—it's his country, his religion, his customs. I don't think I could accept them. I don't think I could live the kind of a life he'd expect me to live." Her gaze met the other woman's. In a quiet voice she said, "Any more than you could, Monique."

The French woman stared at her. Then slowly she nodded and said, "So we turn our backs on the men we love and spend our lives wondering if we did the right thing." The blue eyes clouded with a look so lost, so vulnerable, that Katherine wanted to reach out and comfort her. But she said nothing, only waiting for the moment to pass.

That afternoon, at Monique's insistence, Katherine moved out of her hotel into the house on Rue St. Croix de la Bretonnerie. She'd known Monique for only a few days but it seemed much longer than that. There was a bond between the two women, the bond of being in love with the same kind of man. It was ironic that the men were grandfather and grandson.

The burnt-orange days of September drew to a close. There was a crisp briskness to the air that made Parisians walk at a faster pace and brought color to their cheeks.

Monique's small home was a haven of comfort. Each day Katherine told herself it was time to move on. But still she lingered, hanging on until the last moment to this tie with Rashid's family.

The two women went out occasionally on shopping trips, to a movie or the theater, but most of the time they were content to sit at home in front of the fireplace.

"I love autumn in Paris," Monique said one late afternoon when the sun slanted in through the white starched curtains. "There's nothing more pleasant in the world than sitting in front of a fire watching the colors of Paris turn golden in the twilight." She smiled at Katherine. "Especially when you're with a friend."

"Thank you, Monique. I can't tell you what these past few weeks have meant to me."

"And to me, *chérie*. You are my almost granddaughter. You carry my great-grandchild."

"Monique . . ."

The Frenchwoman closed her eyes. "Have we done the right thing, Katherine?"

"What do you mean?" Katherine's voice was uncertain and troubled.

"We've both left the men we love. Were we wrong? Should we have stayed with them, loving them even though their ways are different than ours? Sometimes I lie in bed at night and I'm overcome with the most incredible feeling of sadness and guilt. I think to myself, well, Monique St. Onge, here you are in this lovely cozy house, in this city you love so much, and you are alone. Is this what you wanted? You have your independence, you have no one to tell you what to do, you may come and go as you please. But you have no one to share your joys or your sorrows, no one to hold you when the nights are cold. What will you do, my fine independent woman, when the snows of winter swirl about you and you are alone in the storm?"

She looked at Katherine, her blue eyes welling with tears. "There have been times, *chérie*, when I have picked up the phone in the middle of the night. When the temptation to call Youssef was so overwhelming that I thought I would die of it. Times when I wanted to cry out to him, 'Yes, I'll wear a veil. I'll stay in my room when you entertain. I'll do anything you want me to do if you'll let me come home.'"

"Then why haven't you?" Katherine asked in a soft voice. "Why don't you?"

The answer was a small Gallic shrug. "Pride. And fear that after all these years Youssef doesn't want me. The last time I saw him—it was eight years ago—I'd have gone back to him if he'd asked me to. But he didn't ask."

"But he loves you! When he told me about you he said, 'Monique is my wife and she'll be my one and my only wife until the day I die.'"

"Then why doesn't he ask me to come back to him?" Monique's face twisted with pain.

"Because he's proud too. The same night, the night he told me about you, he said that he'd never beg you, that he—"

"What? What, *chérie?*"

"He said that he wouldn't beg, that if you ever came back it would be because you wanted to." Katherine's eyes glistened with tears. "That's what Rashid said too. I . . . I guess that kind of pride runs in the family." She tried to laugh, but the laugh turned into a choked sob. When she was able to speak she said, "Don't pay any attention to me, Monique. I've got pregnancy blues. I'll be all right tomorrow."

"You don't feel ill, do you?"

"No, I'm fine. Just edgy. Perhaps a cup of tea will help."

But the tea didn't help. Nor did the light supper Monique prepared. Katherine only picked at her food. The nausea she'd felt in the early months of her pregnancy had abated these past few weeks, but tonight she felt the threatening edges of it and asked to be excused. An hour after she had retired Monique checked on her.

"Are you feeling better, *chérie?*"

"Yes, Monique, thank you. I'm tired, that's all. A good night's sleep will fix me up."

"You're sure?"

"Of course. I'll be fit as a fiddle tomorrow."

But she wasn't. She awoke some time in the night and knew that something was terribly wrong. She tried to sit up but a pain so enormous it took her breath made her fall back.

"Monique," she called. "Monique!"

It took only an instant for the older woman to throw open Katherine's door. "What is it, darling?"

"Something's happening, Monique." Katherine clamped down hard on her bottom lip before she was able to go on. "I think you'd better call a doctor."

"Mon Dieu!" Monique's voice was so low Katherine could barely hear her. Quickly she crossed the room and put a reassuring hand on Katherine's forehead. "You're going to be all right," she said as she picked up the phone. Then she sat beside the bed and held Katherine's hand until the doctor came.

Chapter 17

IT WAS THE LONGEST AND SADDEST NIGHT OF KATHERINE'S life.

The doctor, a short, white-haired man with a cherubic smile, sent Monique out of the room before he examined Katherine. Then, the smile gone, he phoned for an ambulance and told Monique she could go to the hospital with Katherine.

"I'm losing the baby." Katherine wept. "I don't want to lose it, Monique. I want it, I want Rashid's baby."

"I know, *chérie.*"

"Don't tell him."

"Katherine, are you sure?"

"Promise. Promise you won't call him. He'll hate me for this."

"Hate you? Why should he hate you?"

"It's his child. I didn't tell him and now I'm losing it. He'll never forgive me."

"*S'il vous plaît*, mademoiselle," the doctor said. "You must not excite yourself."

"Promise me," she said to Monique.

"I promise, my dear."

The lonely wail of the ambulance siren sounded in the quiet of the Paris night. Through eyes blurred by pain Katherine watched the slow drip of fluid into her arm. She was barely conscious when the ambulance screeched to a stop, only half aware that she was on a stretcher being wheeled down a long empty corridor. She felt Monique's lips against her forehead.

"Don't cry, Monique," she said.

"*Chérie*, oh *chérie*, I'm so sorry."

"Me too."

Then Monique disappeared and Katherine was alone on a high white table under the glare of light. When the light began to dim she whispered, "Goodbye . . . goodbye, baby."

Adrift on a sea of sand. A kaleidoscope of images, shaded by light and shadow, flashed through her mind. The pool at the oasis. Rashid leaning to kiss a drop of moisture off her breast.

Click.

The nomad camp. Abdur and Zahira, hands clasped, dancing around and around.

Click. She and Rashid walking out on the dunes. His burnoose spread on the sand. Moonlight turning his naked body to gold as he looked down at her.

Click, click. The night was dark and she was alone. "I can't see," she whispered. "Where are you? Come back, Rashid, come back—"

"Wake up, *ma petite.*"

"Rashid?"

"No, darling, it's Monique."

"Was Rashid here?"

"No, dear. You were dreaming. But if you'd like to see him I can telephone—"

"No!" She rested her hands on her stomach. "Is it over?"

"Yes, dear."

"There isn't any baby?"

Monique's eyes welled with tears. "I'm so sorry," she said as she stroked Katherine's forehead. "How do you feel?"

"Empty."

"*Alors.* In a few days you'll be able to leave the hospital. You'll feel better when I get you home."

"Monique, you're wonderful. But I can't impose on you any longer."

"Nonsense. You'll stay with me until you've completely recovered. Then you can decide what to do. But for now you don't have to think about anything except getting your strength back." She took Katherine's hand in hers. "It's not the end of things; the doctor said you can have other children. And you will, Katherine. Someday you'll have other babies."

"But not this baby." Katherine squeezed Monique's hand in hers. "I think I want to sleep now," she murmured. Closing her eyes, she put her forearm over them to hide the tears squeezing through her lids.

Katherine didn't accept the job in Geneva. As the days passed she knew she didn't want to stay in Europe, but she wasn't sure she wanted to return to Maine. She also knew she couldn't impose forever on Monique's hospitality. Gripped by ennui, she refused to make plans and was content to let one day drift into another.

When Monique suggested they pretend they were tourists, Katherine agreed. They went to Montmartre to see Sacré-Coeur and to Versailles, where the gardens were resplendent in autumn colors like a Degas painting. They ate in charming little Left Bank bistros and drank wine from the Loire Valley.

They spoke of nothing serious until one night, sitting in front of the fireplace of the house on Rue St. Croix de la Bretonnerie, Monique said, "These past few weeks have been wonderful, Katherine. You've helped me to see Paris through your eyes and I thank you for that. It's been a lovely farewell to the city I love so much."

"A farewell? What do you mean?"

"I'm going home." Monique's smile was self-mocking and gentle. "I'm going back to Morocco, Katherine."

"To Youssef?" Katherine was stunned.

"Yes, my dear. To Youssef, if he'll have me."

"Oh, Monique, I'm so glad. If you're sure it's what you want."

"I'm sure. For the first time in twenty years I feel an absolute confidence in what I'm doing."

Katherine stared at the Frenchwoman. Monique's

announcement had come as a complete surprise. She'd had no inkling that Monique had even thought about returning to Youssef. "What decided you?" she asked at last.

"So many things, Katherine. But more than anything else I think it was getting to know you."

"Me?" Katherine stared wide-eyed at her hostess.

"I saw myself at your age, *chérie*. I saw in you all the love and doubt and fear that I felt when I first knew Youssef. I've been wrong. And forgive me, darling, but I think you've been wrong."

Tears glistened in her eyes as she took Katherine's hand. "We're cowards, Katherine. We're afraid to face how we feel. We haven't had the courage to love. It's almost too late for me, my dear, but you have your whole life ahead of you. Come back to Morocco with me, Katherine, and we'll face those two lions of the desert together."

Katherine took a deep breath, stunned by what Monique had said. Then slowly she shook her head. "I can't. I . . . I really can't."

"Ah, Katherine, you're wrong, so wrong." Monique got up and put another log in the fireplace. When it caught, she turned back to Katherine and said, "All right, I won't say anymore about it. It's your life and you must live it as you choose. But I'm going to ask a favor of you. I'm not sure I can do this alone, Katherine. I need you with me to hold me up in case I falter. It's been eight years since Youssef and I have seen each other. I've changed. I don't know how he'll feel about me. I don't even know if he'll want me back." Her voice trembled. "I'm not sure I can do it alone, *chérie*. Please . . . come with me."

"Monique, I . . ." Katherine hesitated, then caught by the pleading in her friend's eyes said, "All right, I'll go with you. And perhaps . . . perhaps I'll see Rashid. But I won't be pushed—this is something I'll have to decide later. For now I'd rather he didn't know I'm coming."

"Très bien, Katherine. I'll phone Youssef tonight and tell him our plans." With a nervous smile she added, "I'll tell him that I want to come for a visit. Then if he doesn't want me to stay . . ."

"He'll want you to stay," Katherine said. "Of course he'll want you to stay."

"Yes, that's right," Monique said as her hand tightened on the telephone. "A visit. I thought we might leave at the end of the week if that's all right with you."

"Of course it's all right with me." Youssef wanted to reach across the telephone lines and grab her before she changed her mind. Then suddenly he stiffened. "We? Who is we?" There was the sound of a growl in his voice.

"Your Miss Bishop," Monique said, and felt herself relax. So, the old lion was still jealous, was he? *Mon Dieu,* she could barely wait to see him.

"Katherine is with you?"

"She's been staying with me for several weeks, Youssef."

"Good God! Rashid has been going out of his mind. She's coming with you, you say?"

"Yes, Youssef. But please don't say anything to Rashid."

"But, damn it, woman, he's tried every way he

knows to find her. Not that I blame Katherine for not wanting to see him. He treated her shamefully. Shamefully. He's stubborn, willful, determined to have his own way."

Monique smiled into the phone.

"But by Allah he loves her. I'd like to see him have another chance."

"So would I, Youssef. But I've promised I wouldn't interfere."

"Is Katherine all right?"

"She's fine now."

"Now? What's that suppose to mean? Has she been ill?"

"We'll talk about it when I see you."

"And you, Monique? Are you all right?"

"Never better, *chéri.*"

"It's been a long time."

"Yes, Youssef, a long time."

"You'll let me know your arrival time?"

"Yes, of course."

"Call me tomorrow."

"*Très bien.*"

"Call me every night."

"Youssef . . ."

"Say my name again."

"Youssef."

The red city of Marrakesh, pearl of Morocco, city of ancient dynasties, of minarets and mosques, lay below.

Katherine had vowed never to return, yet here she was, gazing out at the red-ochre houses and the palms below. She glanced at the woman sitting beside her.

Monique's face was white and tense, her hands clenched tightly on her lap.

"Do I look all right?" she asked for the tenth time in the last five minutes.

"You look absolutely beautiful," Katherine reassured her. It was true, Monique looked stunning.

The two of them had spent the week before the trip shopping. Katherine had bought only a few things for herself, but it had been fun helping Monique pick out a new wardrobe.

"My trousseau," Monique said with a nervous laugh. "I *hope* it will be my trousseau."

She had chosen a fawn-colored suit for the trip. With it she wore a ruffled blouse of pale ivory, brown high-heeled pumps and a broad-brimmed brown hat. Her hair had been done in the latest French style and her nails were polished a dusty pink.

"You're going to knock Youssef's eyes out," Katherine said as the wheels touched the ground.

"Stay with me."

"I will."

"Every second. Oh, Katherine, now I'm afraid. Am I doing the right thing? Am I?"

"You're the only one who can answer that, Monique. I think you'll know the answer two seconds after you see Youssef."

That's the way it was. One moment Monique was rigid with anxiety; the next moment she cried out, "Youssef!" and began running across the tarmac.

The tall white-haired man stood for a moment watching her, then he too began to run, the long brown djellaba flapping in the wind. When he reached Monique he grasped her arms and held her away from him. Then with a shout he lifted her up off the ground and held her in his arms. On his face there was a look of such utter delight that for a moment Katherine had to look away.

She and Youssef talked all the way from the airport to his home. Monique seemed stunned into silence, suddenly shy as she clasped Youssef's hand.

As soon as they reached the house Katherine said, "I'm terribly tired, Youssef. I wonder if it would be all right if I rest for a bit?" She ignored the alarm in Monique's eyes and the expression that begged not to be left alone with Youssef.

Smiling to herself, Katherine followed one of the servants down the corridor to her room. It was the same room she'd had before and now the late afternoon sun shone in through the apricot drapes, giving the room a lovely look of softness and comfort. She went to stand before the open windows and, drawing the curtains back, gazed out at the Atlas Mountains.

Beyond the mountains lay the Sahara. She closed her eyes and could see the golden dunes of the desert in shimmering light and shadow. She could smell mint tea and horses, warm earth and incense.

When she went into the dining room, several hours later, she saw that a table had been set out on the patio.

"We're out here, daughter," Youssef called. "Monique insisted we dine outside so that she could watch the lights of the city. It's a bit chilly. Will you be warm enough?"

"After Paris this feels like summer," Katherine said. "It's wonderful to be back, Youssef. There's a special scent in the air here in Marrakesh that's unlike anything in the world." She turned to Monique. "Don't you think so, Monique? Is it as you remember it?"

"It's exactly as I remember." The Frenchwoman's smile was warm with happiness.

It was a pleasant meal and when it was over they lingered over mint tea, gazing at the gardens and the city spread out before them. But in a little while, as she had this afternoon, Katherine excused herself so that her two friends could be alone.

After she changed to her nightgown and robe, she opened the french doors and went to stand out on the balcony, breathing in the sweet night air. Below her lay the sweep of terraced gardens. Before she could draw back she saw two figures emerge from the patio. Youssef and Monique, hand in hand, along the green hedges near the rose garden. As she watched, Youssef drew Monique into his arms. He held her for a long moment, then kissed her, a kiss so tender and loving that Katherine felt her heart stand still.

Silently, fearful of breaking the spell, Katherine slipped back into the shadows of her room. Hot tears streaked her face. She dashed them away with her knuckles but they continued to flow. At last she flung herself across the bed and wept her silent tears. Tears for an old love found; tears for a new love lost.

Chapter 18

THE LANDSCAPE OF MOROCCO: OLIVE TREES AND DATE palms, orange groves and wheat fields, robed shepherds tending their flocks as their forefathers had in Biblical times.

From the car window Katherine watched a man, dressed in a dark hooded djellaba, riding a donkey across the dry fields. How little has changed, she thought. I'm the twentieth century, riding in a chauffeur-driven air-conditioned car; he's the good Samaritan riding toward Jerico.

This was such a strange country—so foreign to anything she'd ever known—and yet in less than a year she felt at home here. There was a mysticism about Morocco, a sensuous undercurrent of sights and scents that stirred her as no other place in the world. After this journey to see Rashid she would return to her own land, but she would leave a part of herself behind.

"If you're determined to go alone," Youssef had said, "then Ahmed will drive you. But it's a long drive, daughter. If you'd let Rashid know you're coming he'd send his plane for you. I don't see why you—"

"I'd rather do it this way, Youssef. It may sound foolish, but I'm liable to change my mind halfway there. You see I don't want Rashid to think I'm looking for a reconciliation."

The white bushy eyebrows raised in question, but when he opened his mouth to speak Monique put a cautioning hand on his arm and he said no more.

Now Katherine leaned her head against the uphol-stered car seat and wondered if she were doing the right thing. It wouldn't do any good to tell Rashid about the child she had lost, but in a strange way she felt he had a right to know. Perhaps after this, after she had tied up all the loose ends, she'd be able to put the past behind her and go on with her life. Perhaps in the cold reality of Maine she'd be able to block out the memory of shifting sands and of a man standing naked in the moonlight.

Because it was late and they still had a way to go, Katherine suggested they find rooms in Erfoud. It took her hours to go to sleep and she slept later than she had intended the next morning. It was almost ten when they left for the drive to Rashid's home on the edge of the desert.

Sun glimmered on the endless stretch of road ahead. In the distance Katherine could see the golden dunes, an occasional rider, a few camels.

When finally they turned off the main road her breath quickened. In a little while she saw the palms, then the house.

People stopped to stare when the long black car pulled into the village. Katherine's hands, clenched tightly in her lap for the last few miles, unclenched long enough to wave to a few familiar faces. By the time they pulled up in front of the house a film of perspiration beaded her upper lip.

Fatima came out to stand at the entrance, hands on her broad hips, frowning in puzzlement at the chauffeur who stepped out and around to open Katherine's door. Then, with a gasp of surprise, dark green caftan swirling around her legs, she flew down the steps.

"Marhabán! Marhabán!" she cried, her face alight with a smile as she grasped both of Katherine's hands in her own, jabbering something in Berber that Katherine couldn't understand.

"She says, 'It is a morning of gladness, for at last you have returned,'" Ahmed said.

"It's a morning of gladness for me too," Katherine answered. "Please tell Fatima it's wonderful to see her again and ask where Rashid is."

After another exchange of rapid Berber Ahmed said, "The master went to Bouarfa very early this morning. He'll return tonight. Fatima says she will have lunch prepared and that later you must rest from your trip."

"Shûkrán," Katherine said, trying to hide her disappointment. She'd been preparing her "hello, guess-who's-coming-to-lunch" speech for the last thirty miles. Now she felt letdown and deflated. She ate her lunch while Fatima hovered over her, then followed the Berber woman down the corridor to her old room.

Nothing had changed; it was as though she'd never left. Her comb and brush set was on the dresser exactly as she had left it. The shelves in the bathroom were still stacked with the turquoise and gold towels; the wicker stand still held the bath oils and French soaps.

When she came out of the bathroom she opened the closets. The caftans were there and so were the rows of jeweled slippers.

That evening she bathed, then brushed her hair back from her face and let it flow free down her back. She dressed in a pale blue and silver caftan and matching slippers, and with a slight smile slipped the blue beads that Zahira had given her over her head.

Just as she stepped out of her room she heard the crunch of tires in the driveway.

Slowly, feeling as though she'd never breathe properly again, Katherine went down the corridor to the front entrance. She could hear Rashid's voice, then Fatima's excited shrill of news. His sharp "What? What did you say?"

He looked up then and saw Katherine. For a long and breathless moment neither of them spoke.

I could get lost in the desert darkness of his eyes, she thought. And she was lost, unable to speak or move until he said, "Hello, Katherine. This is a surprise."

She glided down the steps. "Hello, Rashid. I hope my visit isn't inconvenient."

"Visit?" His mouth tightened. "Of course not. How long can you stay?"

"Two or three days if that's all right. I have a reservation to fly out of Casablanca next week."

"I see." His face looked pinched with tension. The strain between them was so taut the air felt rigid.

"If you'll excuse me I'll get cleaned up for dinner." He hesitated. "I see you're wearing Zahira's beads."

Katherine touched them with nervous fingers. "For old times' sake," she said.

He leaned against his bedroom door, eyes closed, hands clenched at his sides. She was here! Katherine was here! He thought he'd been dreaming when he saw her standing there on the steps, all blue and silver, the golden-wheat hair falling in soft waves over her shoulders.

He'd wanted to rush to her, to gather her in his arms and never let her go again. Instead he'd stood there, frozen, barely able to say her name.

She was even more beautiful than he remembered. Beautiful but different. Something had changed her in the few months she'd been gone. There was a new maturity in her face, a touch of sadness that had not been there before. Whatever it was, she was still the most beautiful woman in the world.

But if she had changed, he had not. He still loved her, still wanted her so much that it was agony to be in the same room with her and not touch her.

He rested his head in his hands. Katherine, he thought. Katherine, why have you come back?

They sat at opposite ends of the long dining table and made polite conversation.

Youssef was well. He was delighted that Monique was with him. She, Katherine, had been staying with Monique in Paris for the past month and a half. Yes, Rashid's grandmother was charming. Yes, they'd been to the Louvre. No, she wasn't sure how long Monique planned to be in Morocco.

Katherine pushed the food around on her plate, trying to disguise the fact that she wasn't eating, only too aware that Rashid was doing the same thing.

His face looked so cold, so frozen. She wanted him to reach out and touch her. She wanted . . .

"Would you care to walk in the garden?" Rashid asked when the dishes had been cleared away.

"No, I . . . I think I'll go to my room if you don't mind. I have a bit of a headache."

"Very well. Let Fatima know if you need anything."

"Yes, I will. Thank you."

"I hope you sleep well."

She looked at him and felt the threat of tears behind her eyelids. "Good night," she murmured, aware that her voice was husky but unable to control it.

Once in her room she allowed the tears to fall. Had she been wrong to come, wrong to want to tell him about the baby? She closed her eyes. She'd go back to Marrakesh in a few days. From there she'd fly to Casablanca and then home to Maine. In time all of this would fade, as all dreams must.

When she undressed she opened the drawer that held all of the beautiful nightgowns and selected a gown the color of golden sand. Then she went to stand out on the balcony overlooking the gardens. In the distance she could hear the tinkle of bells and knew that the water seller was making his late evening rounds. The sky was ink-dark blue. A million stars glimmered and glowed. Palm trees rustled in the breeze.

Katherine leaned on the railing, gazing out at the shadowy mountains in the distance. Below her she heard a sound and when she looked she saw Rashid.

Through the half-darkness they stared at each other. Then Katherine turned and went back into her room.

She got into bed, feeling the coolness of the satin sheets against her skin, aware that she was trembling. With a shivery sigh she reached to turn out the bedside light, then froze, her hand on the switch, as Rashid threw open the door.

"What do you want?" she whispered.

"What do you think I want?" His voice was barely controlled. "What do you think I've wanted since that first moment I saw you standing there on the stairs?"

He crossed the room in two strides and before she could speak he gathered her in his arms.

"It's been so long, Katherine," he said against her throat. "So long."

"Rashid, please. I don't think we should—"

"No. Don't say anything. I don't want to listen. I don't care why you've come. I don't want to talk about when you're going to leave. I don't want to talk about anything."

His kiss told of hunger and need and of a desire too long unfulfilled. He devoured her lips, gently forcing them apart so that he could sample the warm recesses of her mouth.

A flame that Katherine thought had been diminished forever flared and grew as his hands explored her body. He touched her with questing eagerness, tenderly, lingeringly, as though he were memorizing every inch of her. With trembling fingers he traced the line of her throat before he moved to each breast.

"Sit up, Katherine," he whispered.

When he had eased the sand-colored gown over her

head he put a hand on her shoulder, forcing her back against the pillows as he pulled the sheet away from her body.

His eyes were hungry as he gazed down at her, his strong nostrils fluted with desire, his lower lip clenched between white teeth. Quickly he tore the white djellaba over his head and stood before her, naked and magnificent, his lean bronze body smoothly muscled, wide of shoulder, narrow of waist and hip, long strong legs apart. His dark desert eyes burned into hers.

When he lay down beside her he gathered her into his arms. His mouth sought hers again, more gently this time as one hand encircled her back and drew her closer.

She thought she'd forgotten the warmth and texture of him, the smell of the desert on his skin. But she'd been wrong; she'd never forget it, never as long as she lived. She ran her fingers over his body. Everything, every line and curve and hollow was as she remembered.

Neck arched back against the satin pillow, Katherine moaned with delight as he trailed a line of kisses down her throat to the hollow of her shoulder. As he drew closer to her breasts she tensed with anticipation.

There was a slow warm flick of his tongue and she gasped with pleasure, then whispered his name as he captured one rigid rosy peak.

Let it go on forever, she thought as she gave herself up to the sweetly tantilizing tongue. Let me keep this perfect moment, let me remember the feel of his lips against my skin.

"It's been so long," she whispered brokenly as she

urged his body closer to hers. "Come up over me, Rashid." Her breath came in ragged gasps. "Please, darling, now. Now."

Burning with longing, her fingers tightened in his thick black hair as she forced his face to hers for a kiss that told him more plainly than words all that she felt. He raised his body over hers and clasped her to him.

When he moved against her, whispering her name in the wheat tangle of her hair, she lifted her body to his. Again and again he found her mouth as his movements quickened and his hands tightened on her body.

Because she knew it would end soon and she could not bear to have it finish, Katherine tried to hold back. He sensed it in the slight withdrawing of her body and slowed his movements, leaning to flick her breast with his tongue. Then it was too much for both of them and their movements quickened, carrying them higher and higher on their sweet flight to ecstasy, up and up, over the peaks and precipices of delight into a whirling galaxy of endless splendor.

Finally, mouths and bodies pressed close, they floated down to quiet reality.

It was a long time before either of them spoke. At last Rashid moved slightly away from her and, smoothing the tangled mass of hair back from her face, said, "How can you deny what is between us, my love?"

"I don't deny it," Katherine said. "I've never denied it. But . . ."

Gently Rashid placed a finger against her lips, silencing her. "I know I'm not an easy man, Katherine. I know there will be problems. But if we both try . . ." He looked down at her. "I won't ask you to cover your beautiful face with a veil or do anything you don't want to do."

He took his finger away and kissed her trembling lips. "We're different people, with different customs and ideas, Katherine, but we can learn to listen to each other with our hearts. I love you—you're my reason for living. I don't think I can exist without you."

"Darling," she whispered.

"I want to marry you, Katherine, to spend my life with you."

His face was freed of all tension now, his eyes warm with a love he no longer needed to hide. "Now tell me what brought you back," he said.

This was the moment Katherine had dreaded. Leaning her head against his chest, she tried to find the right words.

"There's something I have to tell you," she said at last, raising her eyes to look at him. "Something I think you have a right to know."

Dark brows came together in a puzzled frown.

"Perhaps it doesn't matter now, but I think . . . I have to tell you."

"What is it, sweetheart?"

She moved slightly out of the circle of his arms. "I was pregnant when I left here, Rashid."

He stared at her, his eyes widening with disbelief. "What?" Hands gripped her arms like vices. "What are you talking about?"

"I was pregnant. I should have known but I didn't."

"When did you find out?"

"When I got to Madrid."

"Why didn't you return?" Suddenly he froze. Then he ran his hand across her stomach. In an emotionless voice he said, "You said you *were* pregnant."

"Yes."

"You aren't now?"

Slowly Katherine shook her head.

"You didn't want our baby." The painful words were torn from his throat as he thrust her aside, his expression one of utter devastation and fury.

"I did. Oh, Rashid, I did. But I miscarried," she cried out, but she spoke to his back as he strode away. "I wanted our baby." She wept. "I wanted it."

Katherine lay still, staring up at the ceiling with sightless eyes. It was over, she knew that now. He was so angry—he'd never forgive her. She'd hurt Rashid deeply; that hadn't been what she'd wanted to do.

He stood with his back to her and pulled the white djellaba over his head. Without speaking he went out onto the balcony.

Katherine got up. She felt very old and very tired as she slipped into a robe and followed him. I'll go home, Katherine thought. There's nothing here to keep me now. Quickly, before she lost her courage, she said, "I'm so sorry. I was wrong to tell you about the baby. Please believe that I didn't do it to hurt you."

"My God," he said in a voice so low Katherine could barely hear him. "My God, how you must hate me."

She put her hand on his shoulder. "I don't hate you. I know it's over between us and that what I say doesn't matter now, but you have to know, Rashid—you must know that I love you."

She could feel the tenseness of his shoulder under her hand and when still he didn't turn to face her she said, "Rashid? Won't you look at me?"

He turned and she saw his tears.

"Why didn't you tell me when it happened?" he asked in a choked voice. "Did you hate me so much that you wouldn't even let me share your pain? Have I hurt you that much, Katherine?"

"Rashid, no!" She touched his face, soothing the tears away with gentle fingers. "Oh, Rashid," she whispered as she leaned her face against his chest.

They held each other for a long time. Then finally she said, "We'll have other babies. I'll even wear a veil once in a while if it will make you happy. I'll always listen with my heart."

His body trembled with reaction as he kissed her. "Never leave me," he said. "Promise me, Katherine."

"I promise." She looked out at the distant mountains, the sand dunes and the swaying palms. Her arms tightened around him. "I promise," she said again.

If you enjoyed this book...

Thrill to 4 more Silhouette Intimate Moments novels (a $9.00 value)— ABSOLUTELY FREE!

If you want more passionate sensual romance, then Silhouette Intimate Moments novels are for you!

In every 256-page book, you'll find romance that's electrifying...involving... and intense. And now, these larger-than-life romances can come into your home every month!

4 FREE books as your introduction.

Act now and we'll send you four thrilling Silhouette Intimate Moments novels. They're our gift to introduce you to our convenient home subscription service. Every month, we'll send you four new Silhouette Intimate Moments books. Look them over for 15 days. If you keep them, pay just $9.00 for all four. Or return them at no charge.

We'll mail your books to you *as soon as they are published.* Plus, with every shipment, you'll receive the Silhouette Books Newsletter absolutely free. *And Silhouette Intimate Moments is delivered free.*

Mail the coupon today and start receiving Silhouette Intimate Moments Romance novels for women...not girls.

Silhouette Intimate Moments

Silhouette

Intimate 🌑 *Moments*

more romance, more excitement

—————————— $2.25 each ——————————

Silhouette
Intimate Moments

more romance, more excitement

SILHOUETTE INTIMATE MOMENTS, Department IM/5
1230 Avenue of the Americas
New York, NY 10020

Please send me the books I have checked above. I am enclosing
$_____ (please add 75¢ to cover postage and handling. NYS and
NYC residents please add appropriate sales tax). Send check or money
order—no cash or C.O.D.'s please. Allow six weeks for delivery.

NAME_____

ADDRESS_____

CITY_____STATE/ZIP_____

Silhouette Intimate Moments

Coming Next Month

Love On The Line by Anna James

When Dr. Erica Jordan met Josh Ingram "no last names" was the rule—and she was glad. For Josh harbored a grudge against radio advice personality "Dr. Jordan," and the day he discovered her true identity Erica knew that handling her *own* difficulties would not be easy . . .

Island Man by Muriel Bradley

Liana Beldon was determined to save her family's Hawaiian property—only she hadn't figured on their opponent, Jax McHenry. The passion she felt for him clashed with her family loyalties, but she could only hope that this time love *would* conquer all!

East Side, West Side by Jillian Blake

Lane was as chic as her home on New York's east side and as arty as the magazine she wrote for. David Corey was a dedicated doctor, as down to earth as the west side he lived on. Would their love prove the old saying that opposites *do* attract?

Taking Chances by Lynda Trent

Chelsea managed to repossess the wrong car and land an innocent man in jail—but Jason Malone was not displeased. Not only had Chelsea inadvertently given him a lead on his undercover investigation, but she had also presented him with a second, much more interesting target—herself!